The American Dream has dangled before our eyes for over 200 years. The American Dream is the goal that we Americans hold on to when everything else is gone. The American Dream is our ideal.

Too bad it's just a dream.


The Americans Dream
 of marshmallow clouds
 and lollipop lanes
 and TV towns
While the world wails,
 fists clenched,
 eyes blazing,
 tears streaming.

The Americans Dream
 of rocket ships,
 fireworks,
 freedom and alleluia,
While they sleep on
 through the alarm,
 the house afire.

*To Mom & Dad*, Isabel McDowell and Milosh Palecek, to whom the American Dream was real. They did the best they could. Two teenagers who found each other in the South Dakota wind and held on.

Milosh — they called him "Mush" — was first generation Czech. His parents came over from Prague for who knows what reason, lived for a couple years in a boxcar next to town and thought they had it made. When they did move in to town it was in by about a hundred feet.

Isabel's people came from County Cork. She lived with a sister and single mother way before that was common. Her mother waited on Bob Feller the pitcher one time, at the Pheasant Cafe in Winner.

Dad got his big break in getting to go to engineer's school in Chicago for a few weeks and spent part of his career on the Long Pine run, staying overnight at the motel near the tracks and fishing for trout. He brought fish home and maybe a foul ball from the amateur games in Winner when he got a chance to go there on a run and see his brother Jimmy, home from the Pacific war, now with a wife and his own family. Another brother, Albert, served with Patton and later went to South Omaha to work in a box factory. Frank went to California. Molly went away. Dad didn't go to the war because his job with the railroad was considered vital to the war effort.

They said Dad was good enough at shortstop to go pro, but he didn't. Maybe he had to work. Hauled cases at the pop factory before the C&NW. They did the best they could. It's sad, a sad state of affairs for a whole nation. Everyone does the best he can and we end up bombing Hiroshima. Dad cuts the lawn each Saturday morning on his one chance to rest and there go a thousand people in Chile, mowed down by our own CIA. Mom calls us in to supper and poof! Laos is toast. Us kids sneak outside for another round of playing after supper. We play hide and seek, catch lightning bugs, tell ghost stories and leave the screen door open just a peep. A couple hundred intelligent poor people in El Salvador are hustled out of their beds and shot.

# The American Dream

by Mike Palecek

with cover art by Keith McHenry

Published by

CWG Press
1204 NE 11th Ave
Fort Lauderdale, FL 33304

www.cwgpress.com

Printed in the United States of America

5 4 3 2 1

ISBN 0-9788186-0-1

ISBN-13 978-0-9788186-0-9

*Come, Dick.*

*Come and see.*
*Come, come.*
*Come and see.*
*Come and see Spot.*

*Look, Spot.*
*Oh, look.*
*Look and see.*
*Oh, see.*

*Run, Spot.*
*Run, run, run.*
*Oh, oh, oh.*
*Funny, funny Spot.*

— "Fun With Dick and Jane"
[Look and See, 1946]
Scott, Foresman and Co.

# Author's Notes:

As I recall, in the summer 1968, Robert Kennedy came to Norfolk, Nebraska. He was going to speak at the railroad station that these days is a flower planter or native prairie grassland display, I think.

I remember going down there myself, on my bike. I was just out of the eighth grade. I wanted to go to pick a saying out of his talk to live by.

I sat-stood on my banana seat and listened and watched him stand at a podium and gesture with his thumb inside his first finger and I heard that paraphrased Shaw quote that I thought at the time was a Kennedy original:

"... but I see things as they never were and say why not."

Sounds like a plan for someone who wants to try writing novels, I suppose.

At the time I was a pretty mediocre paperboy.

We lived through John Kennedy's murder and Martin and Bobby, barely.

Most of us still breathe.

I remember the night I went to sleep while we weren't sure yet if RFK was dead. My mother said that for him to recover was "what this country needs".

Well, we didn't get it.

Through my adult life I have breathed through a number of presidential elections and watched the Democrats get creamed with such sorry candidates that it was all a person could do to drag himself down the church basement steps to vote and then run home to gargle with Listerine.

Can you imagine what life might have been like with another term of John Kennedy, two of Bobby and two more of Ted?

It would have been unrecognizable sitting next to what we have now.

# Mike Palecek

I didn't go to Vietnam, only because the buzzer went off before I got into the game. I only registered for the draft late due to chronic laziness and apathy.

I went off to seminary at the end of the '70s and then prison, newspaper work, and ran for Congress in 2000. I ran as a Democrat. I was a Democrat because I remembered asking Mom and Dad what we were when Kennedy went against Nixon.

I would have been proud to be a Democrat standing next to Robert Kennedy, but standing next to the big shots of the Iowa Democratic Party on the platform at the state convention in Des Moines made me want to be somewhere else.

These folks did not dare mention war, military, prisons, immigration. Weak and not inspiring and to this day they continue playing the same games.

Back then we believed Oswald did it. We believed in the Warren Commission, Johnny Carson, the Catholic Church, the *Norfolk Daily News*, and the *Omaha World-Herald*, because we were brought up to believe. Go Big Red.

We believed in the network TV news anchors — and anything on radio news was true, of course. This isn't Russia.

Now we have the Internet and we don't believe in any of that stuff — we know they killed Wellstone and did the whole 9/11 thing themselves, actually *stole* elections — but still we drift toward fascism as if on a rubber raft on a lazy Sunday afternoon on the Niobrara River, not having the energy to really care about anything, or even lift up our heads to see where we're heading, just toss the empties into the water and stare up at the sky.

And leave it all to people in Congress who are either cowards or too rich to care or both.

We go to sleep at night without hope.

Bobby Kennedy died.

# The American Dream

If any children, my own perhaps, are trying to get in close and hear what I'm going to say, grab something to live by, they might hear, "What time is the game on tonight? Is this enough beer?" But ... there is still some time on the clock. When we die we will be dead for a long time.

We're not dead yet.

Kids, here is what I think.

We should change the national anthem from that firecracker farce we now have to "This Land is Your Land," and sing all the verses. And we shouldn't stand up like tired robots every damn time somebody plays the other one. And I know you give it all you've got, but you can easily end up giving your "110 percent" for a tyrant, and that just ruins everything, like those young people now serving in the military for George W. Bush.

We shouldn't pay taxes for bombs or prisons.

We should let any Mexicans who want to come here to come on in, this being a Christian nation and all, Wally.

Any bishops or priests or ministers who say war and bombs and whatever are A-OK should be sent out to get a construction job.

Phony bastards.

And the Democratic Party — oh, God, the Democratic Party — should say a prayer and light a candle and do penance and look over those pictures of the folks lining the tracks when they brought Bobby Kennedy's body home.

Stand for something.

Care about something.

Feel something.

Imagine health care and poor children fed and bomb factories bulldozed and prison walls torn down and say "why not".

# The American Dream

# **Prologue**

"I want to splinter the CIA into a thousand pieces
and scatter it to the winds."

— John F. Kennedy

The following excerpts are from an interview with comedian
Mort Sahl in the April 1-15, 1968 issue of The Argo.

---

*Argo:* What's the extent of the conspiracy and why is
the government so desperate to keep the truth from
the American public?

*Mort Sahl:* We have determined that elements of
the Central Intelligence Agency planned the
execution and killed the president. Lee Oswald
attended those meetings planning it. He was the only
non-CIA man at the meeting. And he worked for the
FBI ... we still later find Oswald saying, "I was a
patsy," in the Dallas Police Station. The "elements"
are in the Central Intelligence Agency. They don't
want to lose their power. And they don't want to fall.
It has become government by hoodlum. And I don't
blame them. If I were them, I wouldn't want to fall,
either. I would pull out all the stops, as they have.

---

*Argo:* Why is the truth about the assassination of
President Kennedy the last chance of America for its
survival?

*Sahl:* Because the evidence developed by District
Attorney Garrison indicates that certain people had
to take President Kennedy's life in order to control
ours. In other words, as Richard Starnes of the *New
York World-Telegram* said, the shots in Dallas were
the opening shots of World War III. There's been a
great change in this country since Kennedy. I'm

afraid a great deal of hope was interred with his remains.

---

*Argo:* What is the long hard night that America must go through you've spoken of?

*Sahl:* She has to hang on through a period of the military and the CIA with a blank check trying to sell fascism. If she can hang on long enough, Americans may yet live in the country in which they were born. And that is the country structured by Tom Paine and Tom Jefferson.

---

*Argo:* What is the renaissance following this long, hard night that you also spoke about?

*Sahl:* We'll start pursuing the American dream again. I don't know if we'll ever realize it, but we're supposed to have the right to pursue it. And that's what this country is. It's an active exercise in man reaching his upper limit, as they used to say in the math department. And the renaissance will be that a groundswell of public opinion will flush out the rascals because the CIA has infiltrated every area of our national life. I'm afraid the country they subverted best was the United States ... be they in the various right-wing churches or the Dallas Police Department.

— Perry Adams of The Argo interviews
Mort Sahl at "The Hungry i" in San
Francisco, Monday, March 18, 1968

# The American Dream

# Chapter One

The land is flat, and the views are awesomely
extensive: horses, herds of cattle, a white cluster of
grain elevators rising as gracefully as Greek temples
are visible long before a traveler reaches them.

— Truman Capote, *In Cold Blood*

Cracking shots from the blazing boards of a home on the
Westside made the chirping robins on the Eastside look up
for just a moment before going back to their morning work.

The quiet Homeland streets lay deserted, except for the tired
troops marching back to their homes on the Eastside.

If not for the whooshing of the jets strafing the treetops, the
Westside home might reasonably have been presumed to
catch fire from the early morning heat.

One of the robins on the front lawn of the Sun God group
home appeared to wipe its brow with a wing.

The helicopters and bombers, National Guard trucks and
welders' pickups forged across the tracks after a long night.

Michael M sat on the edge of the sofa in the group home,
hands on knees, clicker pointed at the TV, watching the
promotion for The Home Helper Show.

M mouthed along with the announcer: "Residents of
Homeland! Here is your chance to be on the nationally
televised Home Helper Show! Sign up at any Quicke Shop
during the summer, be at the Homeland Elementary School
Auditorium on Saturday morning Aug. 12, and maybe ... your
family home will be included in the new fall season ... of The
Home Helper Show!

"Get your name in now, must be present to win, and let's get
the lovely young Home Helper crew of experts on the job at
your home for one week and miraculously turn your house
into The American Dream Home."

The announcer crouched and fired both pointer fingers at the television audience.

"The Home Helper Show, making The American Dream come true!"

The local weatherman came on to give the workweek forecast. His forehead was drenched with sweat.

"It's going to be hot, hot, hot," he said. "Hotter than usual for this time of year."

A commercial showed the close-up spread legs of a naked woman, with a cold can of Dr. Pepper on her sweating stomach, for sixty seconds without any audio.

M did not hear around him the commotion of the residents getting ready for the morning drive to work.

Al snoozed on the sofa under a framed photo of Homeland Mayor Dick Heavens, while Joseph and Mickey studied the meal menu for the week, pulling it back and forth between them.

With headphones on her ears, Sanndra waved her hands in front of the big side window, a flight deck crew member waving off the approaching starlings before they crashed against the pane.

A staff member worked on the dishes with Rosey, listening to NPR on the radio sitting atop the refrigerator.

Outside, a scene repeated itself — the same picture depicted on the May calendar above the sink in the group home kitchen: A boy and girl head down the sidewalk, the boy on his bicycle, the girl, hair bouncing, trotting alongside. They pass front porches daubed artistically by the morning sun. And even though you see them from behind, you can tell they are in an anticipatory mode, assured they are headed toward something good.

Underneath the calendar a plaque from one of the parents hung:

**WE MAY NOT HAVE IT ALL TOGETHER,
BUT TOGETHER WE HAVE IT ALL.**

# The American Dream

Another photo of Heavens was tacked above the sink.

"Okay! Let's go!" yelled a staffer coming down the hall. "Okay!"

"Huh?" said M.

A radio sitting on the TV set played Christian music from a local station.

"What?" said M.

"Let's hurry. We've got to get us a move on."

M looked around at the people funnelling toward the hall. He clicked off the TV, pushed off and followed.

Sanndra mumbled to herself — the radio announcer on her headphones was giving the reason troops were called to the Westside last night. Farmland Security agents at the telephone company had reason to believe that the rumored alternative bookstore had been found, harboring a collection of apparently excellent, sharp, artistic photos on a computer of faces at the point of sexual climax and that included masturbation.

"Oh my!" Sanndra smiled, put her hands over her ears and headphones and then her mouth.

M walked in a hurry through the hall, his head down, wiping his brow. The garage door must be open, he thought. It's hot already.

Downtown the green National Guard trucks trudged eastward.

On the electronic sign outside the brick bank, a message scrolled:

**Thank You To Our Troops For Keeping Us Free!**

On the Dairy Queen marquee the sign said:

**Over One Hundred Thousand Evil Doers Wasted**

A worker with a ladder and a box of letters headed out to update the number.

Down the walk a young Hispanic mother hustled along with her child.

The boy pointed up at the worker men. The young mom kept her head down, pulling her child along, licking the sweat that dripped into her mouth, averting her eyes from the troops.

Across the deserted street was the corner bakery run by a French Canadian couple, which had been the centerpiece of Homeland for years. Laborers were high on top putting a new face on the Downtown Chamber of Commerce billboard with ladders and paste and putty knives.

This newest poster showed a giant photo of a smiling Dick Heavens in a blue suit, white shirt, red tie, with slogans in stacked lines at his shoulder:

**Hats Are Caps**
**Work Is Play**
**Goodbye Is Seeya**
**Kinda Is Sorta**
**Streets Are Roads**
**Wrestling Is Rasslin'**
**Lunch Is Dinner**

Back at Sun God Group Home the residents milled in the driveway. "We shouldn't have to go to work on such a nice day," John said to Al, who had his eyes closed and his chin to his chest.

Krystal pointed at the blinking red light above the Homeland water tower, where ladders and pulleys draped and a crew hurried to apply a fresh gray coat to cover the graffiti left behind by the graduating class.

"That's the highest building in town since 4-11," she said to Wilma, who stood next to her smiling and rubbing her hands together as if trying to make a fire.

Sanndra pressed her hands flat against her ears and the headphones, and pushed. She closed her eyes and held air in her mouth in order to shut out all the talk around her.

She held it as long as she could and let it out in a rush.

"Ninety-five!" she shouted, eyes still closed.

# The American Dream

"Okay, move 'em out." A staff member buzzed into the driveway on his red moped, causing a resident to dance out of the way.

M hurried to put on his helmet, pulling the strap tight under his chin. The Blue Dust Metallic Flake Beauty had been given to him in anticipation of Father's Day.

"Whoop!"

"Hya! Ho! Ho!"

"Git, now."

"Git 'long, giddyup!"

M joined the other staff members on their mopeds, one red, one blue, one yellow, circling the residents, beeping their little horns, revving their tiny engines — zmmm!

Each morning, much like cattle on the range, the residents of Sun God Group Home and the four other group homes in town were driven to the workshop downtown.

The social services budget of Homeland had been cut in past months to pay for bullets, guns, uniforms, camo toilet seats, tanks and F-16s. The white fifteen-passenger group home vans had been repossessed by the dealership and converted to prisoner transports for the Homeland city jail.

The group of eleven residents started to shuffle down the sloped driveway to the street, gradually revealing Theresa sitting cross-legged on the driveway, rocking.

"Whoop!"

"Whoop!"

Rosey noticed Theresa and stopped, turned back and pointed.

"Hey, what about her," she said to those nearby.

"She's having a seizure," someone said.

"She doesn't have seizures," said Rosey.

She sneaked a look at the staff and scurried over to Theresa, who had a big grin on her face, rocking.

Rosey leaned over next to Theresa and listened.

She came back to her regular morning drive group.

"What'd she say?"

"She's not going."

"Where?"

"To work," Rosey smiled.

M zmmmed back up the driveway.

"Hey! Whoop! Git along now, you guys, you're fallin' behind. What's she doing?"

"Sitting down," said Rosey and the others.

"What? No. She can't. She has to."

M zmmmed up to Theresa. He leaned over with the moped. Sweat from his forehead turned the cement dark gray.

Rosey and the others could see M's mouth moving. He put down his kickstand and stood over Theresa with his hands on his hips. He moved behind her and squatted like a weightlifter getting ready. He put his hands under Theresa's arms and let out an "oof" to try to lift her, but she did not budge.

Sweat streamed down M's face and arms. His T-shirt was soaked. A dark spot appeared on his brown shorts at the small of his back.

The other two staff members zmmmed up, stopped, flipped down their kickstands and stood behind Theresa with M as she rocked and smiled with her eyes closed.

"What's up?"

"She won't go."

"She has to."

"We've got to join the group."

"She won't."

# The American Dream

"Fuck!"

They all three squatted behind Theresa, who now had her eyes wide open and her mouth pursed with determination.

The three put their arms under Theresa's and pushed off with their legs, straining. M looked down and saw that Theresa's behind was off the cement by the thickness of a piece of paper.

All three let go, straightened and placed hands on hips. They tilted their heads at the sky and squinted, their mouths open, sucking in the hot, close air.

M looked and saw that Rosey and the others in the second group, as well as the eight at the corner, were seated in the street.

"Hey! Hey!"

"Whoop! Whoop!"

M and the others ran over and began shouting, waving their hands to indicate they should all stand up and go to work.

Rosey had her cell phone to her ear, calling friends in the other homes.

The staff leader told M to tell the others they were having problems.

"We'll get there as soon as we can."

"Right."

M zmmmed off, down the street, around the corner, leaning this way and that, a "DH '04" bumper sticker flapping from the license plate holder.

Around the next corner he found the nine residents of Vicious Savior Home seated on the front lawn, arms linked, rocking back and forth and sideways, singing "We are gay, we are so gay ..."

M pulled up and learned from the staff that their consumers had heard from Rosey about the "Sun God Sit-Down", as it

8

was now being chronicled, and were also refusing to go to work for the day.

"Same thing up at Holy Battle," said one Vicious staffer. "And over at Awesome Defender and Wondrous Sailor Man. Someone called. We're going to need help."

M gunned his moped, pivoted on his inside foot and spun around in the driveway, his chin strap unsnapped.

As he zmmmed out of the drive he heard the Vicious protesters chanting, "We're so queer and we're here. She loves me, yeah, yeah, yeah."

M buzzed down the street, head down, throttle hand pulled way down.

He leaned to the right to turn, leaned forward, zinging down the street.

Beside him appeared a green camouflaged truck filled with National Guard soldiers wearing black and green face paint.

He leaned right again, hit both brakes hard, sat and stared at the chaotic scene in the street and the Sun God driveway and front lawn.

The residents were still in three groups: Theresa in the driveway, Rosey and her gang of three at the end of the drive and the other eight just at the corner. All were on the cement, their hands behind their backs and fastened with plastic handcuffs.

They were singing, "There is no god but Allah", "Can you tell me how to get to Sesame Street", "Kumbaya my lord, hmm, hmm, hmm", "We shall not be moved", "I love you, you love me".

Rosey had her eyes closed and was rocking gently back and forth, a knowing smile on her face.

National guardsmen, police officers and sheriff's deputies were gathered all around the clients along with the Sun God staff members, in their white T-shirts with the smiling sun, khaki shorts and white tennis shoes. They leaned over talking to them, on one knee, bending down to assist with red-faced hissing.

Police cars and unmarked vehicles and jeeps and trucks were parked at all angles on the street and in the yard, lights flashing, doors open, radios squawking for attention.

"Whoop! Whoop!" yelled the staff members, making shooing motions.

"You have a program!" one yelled. "You will get a zero!"

"Personal space!" a client yelled back at a staffer in her face. "Get away from me."

"M!"

The staff leader hollered while squatting next to Theresa, sweat engulfing his body, a cell phone to his ear.

"We can't get through to the workshop. Phones are busy. You need to get down there *STAT* and tell them we will be there *ASAP*. Go now! Go! Go! Go! The Sun be with you!"

M wiped his face with his forearm, slammed his light blue flake helmet onto his head, pulled the chinstrap tight, loosened it a touch, then pounced onto his moped. He pressed the auto start red button, revved the motor, rmmmm, used his foot to pivot and took off. He swerved sharply to miss a flushed police officer in a sweaty blue shirt, standing with hands on hips and staring down at Rosey, who was still seated on the warm cement, hands behind her back, eyes closed and a Mona Lisa smile on her lips.

Rmmmm! M leaned left and right and swerved through the mess with a divine purpose.

He headed down the street, passing a line of National Guard trucks. At the corner of Oh, Most Holy Warrior Christian School, M barely slowed to tilt right and turn. He leaned on the throttle and charged right through a blinking red light atop a sign in the middle of the road:

**Do Not Enter Buses Loading.**

# Mike Palecek

M touched his handbrake to miss a squirrel, gunned the engine to beat a turning bus, looked down to his wrist to check the time and saw a little girl.

She wore a frilly pink dress with white shoes and toted a light blue backpack. She had a bright smile on her face and a white ribbon in her red hair.

M recorded it all in the instant he realized he was going to kill the child.

The girl trotted across the street toward the Christian school, her parents on the other side smiling and waving out the windows of a Brand New Shiny PitchBlack Chevy Blow Job, enraptured with thoughts of their beautiful child.

The girl stopped in the road to turn to wave to her parents with her fat fist, heard the zmmm, then looked at M and smiled.

M smiled back.

The girl's father saw that his daughter was going to meet the Sun God right that instant and his mouth froze open and his waving hand spread wide.

M swerved and headed right for the shiny black door.

The father's other hand came out the window in an attempt to ward off the zinging moped.

M clenched his front hand brake. He vaulted forward.

His blue flake helmet smashed the father in the face, sending him back into the vehicle, spewing blood onto the new interior and the mom.

M and his moped bounced back into the street. M's body ricocheted ahead again and his hand stuck on the throttle, gunning the engine. Off he flew behind the BJ.

The little bike vaulted the curb. His helmet slipped over his eyes.

He scattered a gaggle of gray-haired girls sporting new flowered dresses, sending them to their hands and knees.

11

# The American Dream

M careened over the grass headed for the war memorial, an area in the corner of the park with marble statues for each war, plus flags, benches and flowers.

He fought to get his front tire back to earth and threw back his head to clear his eyes.

He smacked the front tire against a white stone bench.

M soared over the handlebars, flying, waving his arms. His mouth and eyes were wide.

He ducked his head just as his blue flake helmet rammed World War II.

# Chapter Two

No man who owns his own house and lot can be a
communist. He has too much to do.

— William J. Levitt

M awoke with a headache.

An out of focus black ant on his nose inched forward and
disappeared.

M felt the concrete on his ear.

He saw the world tipped on its side, his helmet cracked and a
pool of blood under his nose. He wondered if anyone had
seen him.

Maybe he could just get up and nobody would notice. He still
needed to get to the workshop, to notify them the morning
drive would be a little late today.

"Oh, my!"

"He's got a bomb!"

"Call the National Guard!"

"He's part of the sit-down rebellion!"

M pushed himself up to sit.

"I'm staff," he said, just as he saw his moped was on fire on
the lawn.

The maroon World War II marble stone he had hit with his
blue flake helmet had slammed against World War I and
Korea, which were also broken in pieces in the middle of the
concrete pad.

The old ladies in the flowered dresses were pulling each other
up and trying to get grass stains out by sticking
handkerchiefs in their mouths and dabbing, rubbing,
complaining.

13

# The American Dream

M sat back on his hands and watched an ambulance, two fire trucks and a sheriff's unit squeal up in the street.

"Suicide bomber!"

"Terrorist!"

"In Homeland!"

"He tried to slaughter my entire family!" The tall father from the black BJ walked up swiftly, waving his arms.

M heard the sound of dozens of feet stomping. He looked down the street, between the legs of those around him, and saw two lines of National Guard troops jogging his way.

Firemen in helmets and yellow suits, and lawmen with hands on their firearms, sprinted across the lawn toward M. He wiped his nose with his forearm and reached out a hand for a towel or something.

"Down!

"Down!

"Down!"

A large young man with barrel biceps and tight brown shirt and flattop haircut halted just in front of M, spread his feet wide and pulled his revolver, gripping it with both hands. He held it out straight and pointed at M's bloody nose.

"Down!"

M lay back on the powdery cement and chunks of marble, facing the sky, his hands flat against his side.

"I'm okay, really," he told the policeman. "Nothing's broken, maybe my nose."

"Over! Over — over — over!"

M saw the red face above him, blotches on the neck. M rolled to his stomach, his face flat against the cement, lying in his own blood, his hands flat against his sides, his nose on fire.

# Mike Palecek

M heard wap-wap-wap. His hair and the dust on the cement pad blew. Bits of WW II, WW I and Korea rolled onto the lawn.

M heard the trees blowing, waving. The wind pressed on his back and arms.

The green helicopter set down on the war memorial cement pad a few feet from M's head.

"Leader of the sit-down strike!" M heard the policeman yelling to the men from the helicopter.

"Up!

"Up!

"Up!"

M pushed to a squat.

"I'm staff."

Someone gripped him by his arm and pulled him toward the helicopter.

A ring of National Guard troops on one knee circled the perimeter of the war memorial. They leveled automatic rifles at those milling around.

The whoosh-whoosh of the helicopter blades fluttered the flowered dresses, red, green, blue, yellow, orange. The old ladies giggled as they fought to keep the dresses down. Some put one hand on their new gray hair-dos and one on their dresses, which still puffed up over their waists and faces. Revealed were orange, blue and pink panties, and gray pubic hair, one bush shaved neatly into a gray heart.

The men in camo fatigues pulled M onto the helicopter and secured him by straps and harnesses into a seat.

M saw his family at the park playground. His wife, in a long, loose, clean summer dress, braided hair over her right shoulder, pushed one child on a swing while staring at the helicopter door. Another sat in the sand next to her foot.

The helicopter blades whirled faster.

# The American Dream

The wind waves reached M's wife and kids, blowing their hair.

M's wife took one child by the hand, and, knowing the other would follow, turned to go.

M looked down the street and neighborhood and saw three of the group homes, ambulances in front with lights flashing.

As the helicopter buzzed off over town, M leaned to look out the door.

"Careful," said one of his young guards, gripping M's arm.

M saw the post office and the flag on the white pole in front. Main Street was lined with Sun God flags, each yellow smiling sun on a field of whitest white.

There was the playground, and the school where tomorrow his oldest would take part in the Memorial Day program.

The helicopter shot up like a Ferris wheel, leaving M's stomach behind.

He could see the Westside: railroad tracks, car-littered yards, glistening skin of varied tones, shacks and grass huts and adobe. He could see smoldering and burning houses, hovels, troops in the streets. He could see the dead and dying in the gutterless barrios.

Beneath the wap-wap-wap and the shouting of instructions back and forth between pilot and co-pilot, M heard the familiar squealing of the rendering truck making its run through the streets of the Westside, picking up the dead. Feet and hands stuck out the top; blood and intestines oozed down the camouflaged sides, running over the white words stenciled in military font on the sides and door:

**For God, For Country, For Honor**

M leaned back and closed his eyes trying to make his queasy stomach go away. He was not used to this.

He was an average man. He graduated from Homeland Senior High School, married a Homeland girl and had Homeland kids.

He was not ugly or good-looking. His hair was neither dark nor light enough to draw anyone's attention. He wasn't what you would call skinny or fat.

He opened his eyes to try to calm his stomach and looked down on his town for the first time.

He wasn't tall or short.

He hoped nothing he would ever do would be either too great or too terrible. That was what he had strived to achieve his whole life — until this morning when he saw the promotion for The Home Helper Show.

He needed to get word to his wife, so they could get their names in for the drawing at the elementary gym in August. They could maybe get a deck on their home, or make over the kids' room. Perhaps they would install a dishwasher, and brighten up the bathroom and kitchen. If he could talk them into a swimming pool — oh my god — his wife would be happy and his children would have good lives.

The helicopter was now directly over the Westside. The squealing and squeaking of the rendering truck sounded as if it were right below.

M had only been across the tracks once in his life, riding along with his father as he drove the truck. They picked up dead bodies of the lazy people who would not work, who would not learn English, who did not worship the Sun God. Those people would not mow their lawns or wash their cars. Their churches allowed the words of New Testament Jesus – radical, fool, heathen, heretic.

The helicopter cleared the trees and entered a corn and soybeans planet.

M sniffed the sweet aroma of pig shit. He loved that smell. He did not like the smell of cows. He had not told anyone yet, and really had no plans.

They passed over farms.

As the copter hummed over Faith, folks on Main Street shielded their eyes and pointed.

17

# The American Dream

Again they plowed into the country.

M could see out over most of Jefferson County, named by a powerful settler after himself. He'd also named the towns of the county the way a contractor names the streets of a new subdivision after his children: Homeland, Faith, Betsy, Thomasville, Franklinton, Paineburg, Washington.

They passed over Washington and the pilots began checking gauges and flipping switches. The two guards flicked their cigarettes out the door and stopped talking. They snapped and clicked their weapons.

Below, M spied a farm, a compound, with long metal buildings and kennel runs, no shelterbelts. The fields all around were barren, plowed deep and watered, but not planted.

They began to descend, heading for a round pad in the middle of the complex. M's stomach again jumped. He gripped the armrests and stared straight ahead, hoping it would be over soon.

A fifteen-foot drop like an elevator falling caused M to call out.

"Oh!"

Then they touched down, and it was over.

"Thank God," said M to himself.

# Chapter Three

O Lord our Father, our young patriots, idols of our hearts, go forth to battle — be Thou near them! With them — in spirit — we also go forth from the sweet peace of our beloved firesides to smite the foe. O Lord our God, help us to tear their soldiers to bloody shreds with our shells; help us to cover their smiling fields with the pale forms of their patriot dead; help us to drown the thunder of the guns with the shrieks of their wounded, writhing in pain; help us to lay waste their humble homes with a hurricane of fire; help us to wring the hearts of their unoffending widows with unavailing grief; help us to turn them out roofless with little children to wander unfriended the wastes of their desolated land in rags and hunger and thirst, sports of the sun flames of summer and the icy winds of winter, broken in spirit, worn with travail, imploring Thee for the refuge of the grave and denied it — for our sakes who adore Thee, Lord, blast their hopes, blight their lives, protract their bitter pilgrimage, make heavy their steps, water their way with their tears, stain the white snow with the blood of their wounded feet! We ask it, in the spirit of love, of Him Who is the Source of Love, and Who is the ever-faithful refuge and friend of all that are sore beset and seek His aid with humble and contrite hearts. Amen.

– Mark Twain, "The War Prayer"


"My Heavens" or "DH" or "Dickless" is what they called him. Dick was the mayor of Homeland.

He headed down the west side of Main Street. He and his wife took up the whole walk, pushing a two handled, six-passenger, mono-shock stroller bearing the six "H"

# The American Dream

children, each wearing a camo safety helmet as they headed to their daily dental appointment.

Dick, not a tall man, wore a camouflage safety helmet as well, as did his wife. They each wore camo jogging shorts, T-shirt, tennis shoes and socks.

DH also sported a camo jockstrap with protective cup, extra large, outside his clothes. He reached down to adjust it, to keep the cup from falling out.

Man and wife made the sign of the cross and stopped to watch three F-16 fighter jets scream over downtown at rooftop level, headed for the Westside. They waited and gazed into the distance until they heard the bombs hitting their targets.

"They are keeping us so free!" Dick's wife, Jane, smiled.

He nodded and they continued on their walk.

The electronic, blinking sign at the bank showed 101 for the temperature.

They stopped to peruse the front window display of The Sun God Is So Awesome bookstore, and saw ten copies of their pastor's book "Oh, God" in ten wire rack displays. One hundred additional copies lined the shelf down the north wall, and another hundred or more were on the south wall. There was another display of the same book running down the middle of the store.

Dick and Jane moved off down the walk and stopped in front of the library. Dick ran a finger down the outside of the glassed city announcement board to the "Banned" list. He silently read:

**Air guitar**
***Paradise By The Dashboard Lights***
**<u>DaVinci Code</u>**
***Imagine***
**Daytime lawn watering**
**<u>Harry Potter</u>**

He smiled to see "Air drums" penciled in above Air guitar.

They passed six newspaper vending boxes: green, yellow, red, orange, gray, blue. Each contained the same newspaper, with its front page story detailing last night's mission on the Westside of Homeland, the number of the enemy killed, the types of new weapons used.

Dick halted when his wife stopped to answer her cell phone chimes.

"Yes, oh, yes!

"We'll have to do that.

"Yes, yes, yes.

"Uh-huh.

"Oh, do. Do. ... Do!"

She had to yell the last do as another fighter group roared over. Meanwhile Dick had begun to visit with the bank vice-president.

"One game at a time," said Dick.

The man nodded.

"Take it to the next level."

Again the man nodded.

"On the same page."

The man nodded, yet more intently.

"Step up to the plate."

The man nodded with his whole body.

The man squeezed around the stroller, patting one of the kids on his helmet as Mrs. Heavens closed her phone.

They pushed down the walk, heading toward a Mexican family. The father and mother each guided a child by the hand, and the father also carried a young one on his shoulders. The parents were young, barely into their twenties.

Around their necks each of the five carried an identification certificate in a wooden frame. The document had a gold

# The American Dream

American Housekeeping Seal of Approval, and a color photo of June Cleaver in her 1950s frilly kitchen apron saying, "Emilio Rodriguez is a human being."

Each certificate had a three-year expiration date.

The mother pulled a rope wrapped around her bloody young hand. At the other end of the rope was a child's wagon bearing a metal box that contained a dead boy, a rosary and a stuffed teddy bear — the child they were required to sacrifice at the border crossing at El Paso in return for passage of the rest.

"He-llo." Mrs. H. stopped in her tracks and looked sternly into the eyes of the woman, who also stopped, showed the placard around her neck, smiled, curtsied and said, "He-llo," as was required.

"Oh, no, D, the press."

Mrs. H. nodded at a group of men and women on their knees crawling up the walk, each one holding a writing pad and pen, and gritting their teeth. Sweat poured down as they competed, trying to reach the H's first.

As the newshounds got within ten feet, the local barber rushed from his shop and stood with folded arms, not allowing the journalists any closer.

A car squealed to a stop in the middle of Main Street, and out jumped a young woman in business dress who sprinted over to join the barber in blocking the walk.

She stepped over a crying, naked, skinny brown baby. It stopped for a moment, thinking it was going to be picked up, then continued to screech. The woman joined the barber with arms crossed over her chest.

Dick and Jane stopped and stood straight, smiling wide.

One of the female reporters on her hands and knees crawled between the legs of the business woman to snap a photo of the first family and shout out her question.

Another fighter group whooshed overhead.

The reporters and the Heavens froze until the rockets' red glare, seconds later.

"Mayor Heavens!" she shouted.

"American Pie."

Dick smirked and pointed at her, with her face caught for a second in the undergarments of the business woman.

"How long will the ban on daytime lawn watering last?"

Dick put his thumb inside his forefinger and gestured.

"Soon," he said.

Dick pointed at a male reporter between the legs of the barber.

"Community College, what's on yer mind?"

"Yes ... Mr. Mayor ..."

The baby sucked air into its lungs and let out a desperate cry.

"You have said you would address library fines, loose dogs, dandelions and season pool pass prices. When will we hear something about those matters from your administration?"

Dick smiled, gestured with his thumbfinger and began to speak.

The baby fell to its side and tried to call out. Spittle ran from its mouth. With a mighty effort it rolled to its back, raised its arms for its mother and let out a wail that was drowned out by the roar and suck of an F-16 screaming over.

The pilot gave a thumbs-up as the baby's breath ceased.

"Okay, thanks, seeya," said Jane.

The reporters got off their stomachs, turned and scribbled on their pads as they crawled away.

The Dick and Jane family strolled along.

They passed in front of the brick Homeland jail.

Lined up along both sides of the walk, sitting against the building and on the curb, were women and children with some men mixed in. Heads down with eyes closed, sucking breath, their shoulders drooped as they sat smoking, crying and moaning.

Dick and Jane squeezed between them, forcing those against the wall to pull their legs to their chests.

Inside the walls, as Dick passed on the left within two feet of the cellblocks, came the cries of those inside. Fingernails scraped on the concrete blocks as they tried to reach their children, whom they had bounced on their knees the day before, and whom they would not be able to hold again until those infants were young men and women.

Many of the inmates were Doug Offenders. The War on Dougs had been one of Dick's most successful programs. He and his advisors, notably his wife, had decided that Dougs were ruining Homeland. Now almost all of the Dougs had been arrested and sentenced and sent away on long prison terms.

Next the first family stopped into Homeland Dental Office.

"Hi!"

"Hot enough?"

"Never enough."

"Tenth anniversary!"

"Congrats!"

The radio on low volume behind the counter said something about the number of dead on the Westside in the past week.

"Ford? Chevy?"

"Red?"

"Yellow."

Boom!

Blood splattered over the front window as a policeman squashed someone's head.

An assistant wheeled the Heavens children back for their checkup.

Dick and Jane sat in one of the plastic primary colored chairs by the window, reading books about their family.

The windows shook as if they might shatter when a bomber roared overhead.

"The kids?" one of the women behind the desk hollered over.

"Busy?" Jane yelled back.

"Great, great, great," said the person now invisible behind the high counter.

"Always," shouted Jane.

Blood, thick and maroon, ran under the front door, spreading across the room. Dick moved his feet back to avoid it getting on his shoes.

The rendering truck roared by on the side street next to the office. The driver fought to obey the stop sign on the hill, tune her radio and keep from rolling back. She couldn't see if anyone was behind her.

A black baby body plopped off the side, hitting the pavement with a soft melon thud.

Out the back end a thin young naked woman and an old lady without shoes dropped, cracking their lifeless heads.

The truck roared away, the driver pleased to have found a song she really liked.

The Heavens children were pushed out by the dental assistant and hygienist.

"See you tomorrow!" the women smiled and waved.

Dick and Jane stood.

"See you at church."

"Bye-bye."

# Chapter Four

When fascism comes to America it will be
wrapped in a flag and carrying a cross.

— Sinclair Lewis

They say I'm stupid.

I'm really not.

There's things I understand and some things I have trouble
with.

I know about Homeland and Dick and Jane and all that. When
I was at home my parents made me read from the
newspaper, out loud, every morning at breakfast. And then
we'd talk about it, the stuff I read.

They said I needed to work to overcome my disability. It was
good to read probably, but before that I didn't really know I
had a disability, or what that word meant.

That's one thing I didn't ask them or didn't talk about. I found
out about that on the sidewalk on the way to school.

And I don't want to talk about it now, either, thank you very
much.

So, I know all about city councils, and government and war,
and Barney — big purple goof-off.

When they arrested us that morning they hurt some people.
Some they didn't hurt. They didn't hurt me.

They tied us up, with plastic like six-pack wrappers on our
wrists, and they took us past the jail and slowed way down, to
scare us, and then over to the workshop. They called us in,
through the day, into private rooms, and asked us if we were
terrorists and who our leader was.

I know T. said her leader was M because she has a crush on
him.

26

# Mike Palecek

And the guy talking to me asked me what I knew about 4-11.

I knew quite a bit. He wrote it all down.

I talked a long time. I didn't feel much like working.

I told him I knew it was two remote control planes that struck the grain elevators and how they were exploded down on purpose.

They say the Westside did it, but Dick and his people did it on purpose.

My dad says they got insurance money for it and a bunch of other stuff. He heard some guys putting bets on it at the cafe before it ever happened.

It's all about corn, is what I've heard.

The guy wrote that down too, and then he loosened his tie. He was sweating like a pig.

He even gave me a cigarette and we both smoked in that room. You can't smoke in there though.

He asked me if there was anything else.

I told him there was a lot.

But I had to pee and we were having sub sandwiches for lunch, which I was not going to miss, no way, uh-uh.

But, I said, I'll tell ya this one more thing, and you make sure you write this down. I pointed right at his yellow pad.

They say all this bombing, arresting and putting on six-packs is to preserve the Homeland way of life.

Well, just what is the Homeland way of life?

Watching TV and eating.

And for that we kill people and let little kids starve and torture people and put them in jail.

I think T. was right to sit down in the street.

She was just havin' a "behavior" they say, but there's more to it. She's not stupid, either.

# The American Dream

She knew that every minute she was sittin' on her butt in the driveway was one minute she wasn't spinning nuts onto bolts.

Nuts. I got their nuts.

I got their nuts.

I am stupid, though.

I know. They gave me tests when I was little and then I had to go to retard school. I know what that means.

And I'm probably wrong as usual, but you asked me what I thought.

That's what I think.

I told him again I had to pee and he was still writin' when I left.

# Chapter Five

"Gee, Wally."

— "Leave It To Beaver"

"Hoss went to town."

— "Bonanza"

"Marshal Dillon went to the saloon."

— "Gunsmoke"

These three television shows were watched by millions of American households each week in the early 1960s prior to the Kennedy assassination.

Some interesting statistics:

According to the A.C. Nielsen Co. (1998), the average American watches 3 hours and 46 minutes of TV each day (more than 52 days of nonstop TV-watching per year). By age 65 the average American will have spent nearly 9 years glued to the tube.

Hours per day that TV is on in an average US home: 7 hours, 12 minutes

Number of TV commercials seen by the average American by age 65: 2 million

Percentage of Americans who can name The Three Stooges: 59

Percentage of Americans who can name three Supreme Court Justices: 17

# The American Dream

NEW YORK, September 29, 2005: Nielsen Media Research reported today that the average American home watched more television the past TV season vs. any previous season. During the 2004-05 TV season [...] the average household in the U.S. tuned into television an average of 8 hours and 11 minutes per day. This is 2.7% higher than the previous season, 12.5% higher than 10 years ago, and the highest levels ever reported since television viewing was first measured by Nielsen Media Research in the 1950s. During the Sept 2004-Sept 2005 season, the average person watched television 4 hours and 32 minutes each day, the highest level in 15 years.

The next morning birds chirped and the sun shined bright.

Students on foot bounced along the sidewalks, headed for the Memorial Day ceremony and the last day of school.

Old veterans in small groups climbed into Buicks, and younger loners fitted on their narrow caps with both hands and checked underneath before getting into pickups.

Old ladies touched starched hair before setting off down the front porch steps.

The Dick Heavens clan promenaded down Elm Avenue, slipping in and out of perfect shadows and light.

They were approached by a neighbor man on his way home from a morning walk.

"H'lo." The man stopped. "Could rain."

"Yep."

"I've seen it come down hard in May."

"Yes."

"At least it's not snow!"

"That's for sure."

"You folks have a good day!"

"Seeya."

Tom Otherfield, band director, worked hard at getting the chairs on the gym stage just right and the goddamn tubas in a straight line in back. He checked the microphone and hurried off to pee.

In the boys restroom Otherfield towered over the urinal.

He forgot to tuck in his shirt, and just sprinkled water on his hands to keep from erasing the notes he had written. He swept his moist fingers through his unruly hair in a cursory attempt to subdue it for the moment.

In front of the school, kept in a remote square at the school corner by yellow crime scene tape, a group of first graders held handmade posters:

**No Blood For Corn**
**Not MY Mayor**
**4-11, What Really Happened?**
**Fraud**
**Murderer**

The crowd filtered in by the school front door, casting disgusted glances at the free-speech zone group that was shouting and chanting from the end of the block.

The people settled into the seats filling the gym floor. The Heavens family sat in the front row, off to the left, and Mayor Dick took his chair on the stage with the principal, Carol "Soup" Campbell.

Tom Otherfield stood in front of the band, waiting for his signal from the principal.

The stage and the gym were lined with Homeland Sun Flags on poles, all around the stage, up and down both sides of the gym and down the middle.

Specially assigned honor roll eighth graders were allowed to light matches from designated spots around the gym, to get the smell of gunpowder in the room.

# The American Dream

Veterans of all the wars were escorted and wheeled and dragged up to a section of reserved metal folding chairs, in front on the right-hand side.

The grades were seated in groups in assigned, square sections, with the adults finding spots to plop wherever they could.

The principal stopped talking to Dick Heavens, raised her chin and almost looked toward Otherfield, who lifted his wand while keeping his eyes glued to her. She was watching to make sure that all the adults and veterans had found a place, that the volunteer ushers from Wimps Without Wars had propped open the back and side doors, and that all the adults had an "Our Mayor Dick" fan with a color photo on its face, to cool themselves.

The principal smoothed her dress and stood to walk to the microphone in the middle of the stage.

"Welcome. Today we honor those who have given the ultimate sacrifice — a disruption of their daily routine — in order to root out those who hate our bone-crunching thighs."

She turned rock solemn.

"Please remove your pants to honor Homeland."

As the children and adults dutifully dropped their pants and skirts, the principal looked at Otherfield and nodded.

T.O., as the kids called him, jerked his head to his student band, raised both hands, whispered something-something to them with wide mouth and bounced his wand one-two-three.

The strings and winds and percussions and what-else began to play.

"Ohhhh, say, does thaa-aat ...," Campbell sang in a plucky alto.

The fans beat back and forth and toes tapped.

A portion of the second graders fidgeted and looked at each other.

"... that our colored piece of cloth was still there ..."

The old veterans nodded.

The younger ones fidgeted and looked around the room for cigarettes to borrow.

"... hanging on that ... one pole thing ..."

Dick Heavens smiled and gave the thumbs-up to his six children.

"... by the top of the roof thing!"

The cymbals clashed and the tubas bellowed.

The crowd applauded and some old vets blew wet farts as they awakened in a start.

The principal pulled up her pleated dress, balancing by holding the microphone firmly with three fingers.

"We are proud today to have with us someone who gave his life for us, for our freedoms, our ability to study and worship and work in peace, not bothered by others, by their problems and desires — so that the people of Homeland might live as the Sun God deigned, in prosperity and comfort and a profound lack of curiosity that really has not even yet found its full depth. For this we are thankful today."

The people applauded politely while keeping the fans waving as well.

The principal nodded and four young Marines in full dress uniform marched up the middle aisle: blue suits, medals, tassels, white high-top boots, white gloves, white hats.

The chunky drummer gave a rapid rat-a-tat to accompany their marching boots on the hard polished gym floor.

Each of the Marines held out in front of him a glass vial that he placed smartly in a vial holder case thing from the eighth grade science lab, on a table below the stage, in front of the crowd and the town.

"We are pretty certain," said the principal, "that this is the DNA, or something resembling it, of one of the original inhabitants of Homeland. Of course it wasn't called that then," she smiled, and the sweaty crowd smiled politely with her.

# The American Dream

"Here lie the maybe remains ..."

She moved away from the microphone to stand above the vials and point down to each one in turn.

"... of the left hand, right hand, nose or maybe left ear, and right foot ... member of the Pleistocene caveman tribes ... person ... fought against what we believe was a tribe trying to take away their freedom to take their land if they wanted."

"This man — or — woman?"

She looked up at her audience and quizzically tilted her head.

"Fought to preserve freedom and Homeland! And all that stuff we talk about!"

The hundreds of fans in the hot sauna of a gym stopped flapping their fans. Everyone held their breath. The veterans remained seated, but swiveled their legs left and snapped a salute to their brows.

The principal raised her hands to her mouth, together, as if praying, and looked down at the vials.

She closed her eyes and counted inside her head to one-thousand three.

She opened her eyes, put her hand over her heart and recited, along with the crowd.

"These colors don't run.

"Good to go.

"Stay on the same page.

"Speak English.

"Amen." The principal briskly returned to the microphone.

"And now I would like to introduce to you a man who needs no introduction ..."

The fans waved feverishly. The second graders swallowed their Adam's apples.

"Our Mayor! Our Homeland! Our Dick!

"Heavens!"

The people applauded and fanned, and looked to make sure that every damn available window and door had been opened.

"Thank you, principal, thank you."

He smiled at the veterans and vials, and gestured with his thumb tucked inside his pointer finger.

"You know ... "

The second graders in the first row of their section looked at each other and then away.

"Our greatness begins at the supper table. Some would have it called dinner ..."

One second grade girl took the bow out of her hair and let it fall over her shoulders. She shook it.

"...but let us not be fooled by imitations of the terms and things we have been told are true.

"That is where respect and learning take place, and where our children come to truly memorize and copy the rituals that we have ..."

On a nod from the girl who had removed her hair bow, the first row of second graders stood together.

They grabbed their red and white Homeland Elementary T-shirts and pulled them over their heads to reveal black ones. White photo outlines of Dick Heavens framed the words:

**Worst Mayor Ever**

In unison they turned their backs to the mayor and stood, eyes straight, not responding to the calls of the adults to sit down and turn around.

"Uh, and, when ... we, uh, eat," Dick continued, "we pass, along with the peas, our values, and, uh ...

"*Do* something with those children!" He held his right arm out straight and pointed at the second grade dissidents. "They should be practicing their desk dives, not out protesting. That

# The American Dream

doesn't do any good. You are protesting at the wrong place, people!"

Most of the adults continued to fan themselves and stare impassively at Dick on the stage.

He searched the room for some response to his demand. He stepped out in front of the microphone to stand with his toes over the stage edge.

The old veterans sat with crossed arms looking up at him. The younger ones studied the floor.

The second graders gritted their teeth and clenched their fists at their sides, waiting for the smack on the head or butt, or the shot between the shoulder blades.

Dick returned to the microphone.

He finished his speech and sat down.

The band played another number.

The Marines marched out with the oldest veteran vials, followed by the veterans in wheelchairs and with walkers. Behind came the able ones, and the younger ones, with searching eyes scanning the floor for cigarette butts.

Then the band on the stage marched out, followed by the smiling principal and mayor.

The second graders screamed, threw up their hands and hugged each other.

The adult crowd followed the students out the front gym door, sweating, clutching their chests, panting, holding on to each other, trying to make it to the door, a wavy mirage a hundred miles away.


Outside, a cool breeze touched each person on the cheeks, congratulating them for making it through the ceremony.

The children began to chase each other and strip to the swim suits beneath their clothes.

The adults visited, causing a traffic jam at the doorway.

The principal and Dick were joined by the Heavens family on the sidewalk. They did not at first notice a circle of children that had formed around them.

"Yes, oh, yes," said Jane to the principal.

Dick looked down on the interlopers.

The six Heavens children waited silently in the stroller beside their parents, staring straight ahead.

"Yes, yes," answered the principal.

"Going to be hot," said Dick, wiping his brow.

"That's good," said Jane, looking at Dick and then the principal.

"One, two, three, four, we don't want your stinking war!"

The group of kindergartners around the Heavenses and the principal began to chant. They held hands and closed their circle tighter, as they had practiced.

> One ... two, three, four.
> One, two ... three, four.
> One, two, three, what're we fighting for?
> Don't ask me, I don't give a damn,
> The next stop is Viet Nam!

"Viet Nam?" Jane looked at Dick. "Oh, dear! Not Viet Nam! Oh, Dick, Oh, no!" She clutched her chest.

He shrugged his shoulders and frowned and looked down the walk.

One, two, then three sheriff's deputies in tight brown shirts ran up to part the circle of kindergartners, grabbing Dick and Jane and the principal to spirit them out of the way.

The kindergartners sat in their circle and continued to chant.

The heads of three snipers in face paint appeared on the top of the roof. The Heavens family was hustled into the school, to the principal's office. The thin barrels of the sniper rifles poked over the roof edge.

# The American Dream

One deputy helped the Heavenses and the principal to the floor of the office, under the table. Another two deputies stood outside the locked door talking into headsets, shotguns across their chests.

Tom Otherfield sprinted down the hall from the band room, tie and coattails waving, his long arms and legs flailing as if he were trying to fly, anything to go faster. He hit the steel push rod on the outside door with both hands and jumped at the roar of a chorus of rifle shots outside.

The band director banged the door open.

He smelled gunpowder.

He saw four kindergartners lying on the sidewalk turning red. One boy was on his back, his arms out, his face gone. Another boy lay on his side, his arm over his head as if trying to hide the hole where his ear had been. Two girls stretched out face down on the cement, their arms out as if flying, the backs of their heads a tangled, maroon mess of hair and blood and brain and bone.

The other children cried and tried to hold and comfort their dead friends. Adults ran back and forth and jumped up and down, crying, screaming, holding their mouths open in silent horror.

Otherfield rushed into the middle of the exploded circle and knelt over the two dead girls. He then picked up one of the boys in his arms. Tears ran down his face.

He looked up to the empty rooftops and all around, searching for an ambulance or police officer or sheriff's deputy to help his students.

The smoke cleared and Otherfield noticed the sounds of birds chirping and the roar of trucks. Around the corner he saw a National Guard troop carrier, followed by another one.

# Chapter Six

"My dad died for that flag!"

"Really? I got mine at K-Mart."

— Bill Hicks

That Sunday Dick and Jane and the family strolled down their walk wearing "hunter's orange" suit, dress, and dress-up summer shorts with their camo helmets.

They walked through their tree-lined neighborhood, enjoying the music from the windows.

Jane sang along as she pushed the stroller, "Our Sun is an awesome Sun ..."

The neighborhood radios handed the Heavens family off to the pre-service organ music streaming from United Sun God Reformed Church.

On top of the church on the corner, on a stout metal pole, flew a huge Sun God flag that once soared proudly above the car dealership on the highway. It waved in the breeze, rippling perfectly, back and forth.

Two long, gently winding sidewalks, lined with plants and flowers, connected the church front steps to the walks on either side of the building. Small white crosses lined both sides of the walks, and scattered in the grass were baby dolls with red paint smeared on them. Arms and legs had been removed. Nearby, overturned, were several children's toy wagons.

# The American Dream

A glassed-in bulletin board in the middle of the lawn told the time of services and gave Pastor Steve Cash's saying for the day:

**The Sun God says: "Save Your Money. Secure a Comfortable Retirement. Stay on the Same Page."**

A sign on the anteroom bulletin board, in colored crayons said:

**Oaxaca Desert Oyster feed**
**"Illegal" Mexican nuts**
**Money To Go To the Summer Bible School Mission Trip**

The Heavens walked down the middle aisle to their seats in the front row, on the left, in front of the lectern.

They greeted those around, and unbuckled and removed their camo helmets. The kids began watching the tiny TV screens attached to the pews, listening by the headphones provided.

Dick and Jane sat down, took deep breaths and smiled, gazing up at the mural covering the wall behind the altar. A tight, white T-shirt showed large breasts and the Sun God flag with the slogan "One Nation under God".

The congregation waved Sun God fans, and looked to make sure each stained glass window was open at least a crack. The windows showed scenes of Jesus slaying the dinosaurs.

The organ began to play. The congregation rose to sing, then sat as Pastor Steve approached the lectern.

He smiled.

He nodded.

He closed his eyes, took a deep breath, held it and let it out.

Pastor Steve opened his eyes and gripped the sides of the lectern.

The congregation rose as one. They raised their hands into the air, shook them, then brought their arms down and lowered their heads, keeping their arms out straight, keeping their hands waving.

"Boom chucka lucka-lucka boom chucka," they moaned.

"4-11 is on our minds and hearts. Since 4-11 ... there can be no more 4-11s. If we recall 4-11 and be vigilant about the last 4-11 ... keep it always in our minds."

Those near the aisle fell onto their stomachs, stretching out their legs and arms as if belly surfing, shaking their hands, moaning, "boom chucka lucka-lucka boom ...."

"Amen."

Pastor Steve asked his people to rise or straighten up and open their bibles.

"Please turn to the Gospel of Luke."

Each of the bibles had been blacked out, leaving only the articles.

"Please recite along with me the words of our Savior," said the pastor.

"A, an, the, the, the, the, an, a, an, a, a, a ... the.

"Amen."

"Amen."

"Praise be the Sun God," he said and raised his hands, pressing them down as if pushing on their heads to make them sit.

"We are happy for this warm weather," he began in a stentorian tremor.

"Warming is right and good. The Sun God is good and loving and warm. This world must end, should end, will no doubt end, at some point ... and the righteous, the lovely, the saved, will join in Sun God paradise, for ever and ever.

"We shall drink and keep drinking, rest and stay sitting, eat and continue eating. "

He paused and smiled while looking down, then addressed the congregation sternly.

"The Evil One, Michael M, has been captured by the forces of rightness and good and warmth. That is good. That is right. We must guard against terrorism and homos, against those

41

who would seek to do us harm, to take away what is rightfully ours: Our Stuff.

"It *is* our stuff! And praise the Sun God we have the bullets and banks and employers and police and courts and jails that will help us to keep it. They will, by God, or they will be out of a job and will be in jail themselves, or such outcasts in their own families and neighborhoods that they will get very depressed. Not being able to pay for food or cars or water or electricity, and having no real skills, they will look at the Help Wanted ads and wonder where in hell they fit in, and *wish* they were dead. So help us, God. Amen."

"Amen."

He poured himself a glass of ice water from the pitcher on the marble table next to the lectern and took his time drinking it, sending out individual smiles around the church as he swished and swallowed.

While holding the glass, he added conversationally, "You know, we know what phone calls Mr. M made to organize the riot and the sit-down. We know what books he took out from the library for research, and we know what videos he checked out. Michael M rented 'The Big Lebowski' one hundred ... uh, eighty one times. Doesn't that strike you as a little odd? What kind of man *does* something like that?"

He put the glass down, touched his red tie and his white shirt and blue suit with his elegant hands and became serious again.

"Yesterday we celebrated Memorial Day, and those who have slaughtered in order that we might be comfortable.

"It is right and good that we do so, as we do on all of our patriotic days: Flag Day, Loyalty Day," he counted each one out on his long reptile fingers, "Veterans Day, Armed Forces Day, Save Your Own Ass First Day, Scattered Guts and Teeth Day, Dripping Layers of Burnt, Crisp Brown Skin Day, Squashed Foreign Infant Eyeballs Day."

He folded his hands into fists.

"It is right and good and warm to have traditions. They tell us who we are, where we are going. They give us steady passage in rough seas, times of trouble.

"For this we are thankf ..."


Jane excused herself to Dick and those around them, to take the children to the rear.

They entered the glassed-in exercise room that covered the back of the church. They changed in the dressing room and came out to join the other moms and children, to watch church and ride exercise bikes or work on stair-steppers or treadmills.

Jane put each of her six children against the wall with the other young ones, and snapped their wrists and ankles into primary colored, hard plastic locks. She stuffed a clean white and yellow Sun God handkerchief into each of their mouths and went to ride her favorite Exorcisor.

She began visiting with the moms around her as they watched a TV in the corner of the room.

They visited about children and their husbands and exercising.

They talked about money and their homes.

"At least we're getting our bills paid," said Jane, "that's what's important."

The mom on the bike next to hers nodded while peddling and watching the TV.

"Yeah. Not much else you can do. Just keep trying, keep going."

On the TV, skinny African children were sitting on hard dust, staring at each other with bug eyes, flies on their mouths.

# The American Dream

Pastor Steve motioned toward Dick, in front of him, then back to Jane on the bike and their children attached to the wall.

"We are so grateful to have candidates that recognize our values," he said. "In the coming elections I hope you will support them. They need us. We need them.

"It is by the faith of Mayor Dick Heavens that he has been able to survive these past difficult years. He and his administration have given us the Freedom Fondler's Act; HomeTown Lockdown; Most Children Behind; Clean Skies; Thick Forests; Flat Roads; Longer, Stronger Sex; and Breasts! Breasts! Breasts!

"For this we are thankful.

"Now, let us pray."

He raised his arms and brought them up.

The congregation began to sing.

In the workout room Jane realized that the intercom was turned off. She climbed from her bike and went over to switch it on, and turned the TV volume down while she was there.

She went back to riding her bike and visiting with her neighbor.

The women heard the men in the church coughing and rustling papers.

The microphone squeaked and someone dropped a songbook.

"And now," said Pastor Steve. "We are proud to bring up someone who is one of us. Someone who has served in our military, helping to bring freedom to our homes and vehicles.

"Please welcome Lance Larsen, produce manager at 'Too Much Food' and staff sergeant in the Homeland National Guard. Lance?"

# Mike Palecek

Dressed in camouflage fatigues and cap, Lance Larsen walked from the front row on the right side up to the lectern in front of him, opposite Pastor Steve's.

He made the sign of the cross and began talking about how his unit was patrolling the Westside on a recent night, searching for terrorists and as always trying to find the bookstore.

"We went to the door of these suspects, knowing it would make everyone more free-er ..."


Jane began to pull her T-shirt over her head. Out plopped her large breasts, already at attention.

With her palms she massaged her excited pancake-type nipples as she approached her neighbor on the exercise bike, who was riding with no hands in order to remove her sweaty pink top.

"We pointed our weapons and hollered at the tops of our voices in order to be understood ..."

Keeping his eyes straight ahead, watching Pastor Steve massaging his own nipples through his shirt while he listened to Sgt. Lance Larsen speak, Dick reached his right hand over to the bank vice-president sitting next to him.

With a practiced style, Dick undid the man's pants, reached inside and found his ready log. He squeezed, not too hard, then squeezed again, gently milking the breathless banker.

"The women and children had these big, creepy bug eyes, and they wouldn't close their fucking, sorry, mouths, and we stuck our *fucking* barrels right inside their teeth and told them to suck it if that's what they wanted ... they just kept looking at us like they was scared to death. All we was there was to make our friends and family free back home. A friend of mine shot this one kid ..."

Jane took her next-door neighbor's immense breasts in her two hands and caressed them, then squeezed them, hard.

45

# The American Dream

She then put one almost entirely into her mouth as she ran a hand to the crotch and stuck three fingers all the way inside her neighbor. Her neighbor lady moaned, sucking Jane's blonde hair. Jane forced in a fourth finger.

Pastor Steve had his penis sticking out of his pants, and was running one hand up and down while keeping the other hand pinching his nipple. With wide mouth he looked out over his congregation as the men in the church worked on each other, rocking, moaning and screaming out. The ladies in the exercise room, with one ear pitched to the intercom, delighted each other with inspiration.

"The head and hair and blood just sprayed out the back of the kid's head. And I was so proud," said Lance Larsen. "Because I knew how free I would be when I got home to attend the church of my choice."

Dick leaned down to his right to take the bank vice-president into his mouth. The VP rubbed the top of Dick's head and watched Sgt. Lance Larsen, tears streaming down his cheeks.

Jane now had her neighbor on her back on the exercise room carpet. Jane stuck her face into her neighbor's crotch and licked and shoved her nose inside.

She clutched her next-door neighbor lady's bottom with her yellow-painted fingernails, leaving ten puncture holes and a blood-spotted thin green carpet. Her neighbor opened her legs yet wider and arched her back, putting her hands flat on the floor and bridging, while listening to the words of Lance Larsen.

"The lieutenant gave the sign, and we pulled back out of each other's way and shot the rest of that family. The dad and the brothers in back, too, who wouldn't talk, just stared at us, so we shot them first, about a hundred times. It was good, felt like we at least did something that night, not just ride around.

"That whole little house was full of blood, running down the steps, the sidewalk, into the street. I shit you negatory — sorry. Saving freedom, that's what I love. That's why I signed up. I'd do it again, knowing you people are behind me. The Sun God blesses you."

Pastor Steve zipped his pants, ran his hands through his hair and put both hands on the podium. He wiped his hands down his pants and rubbed the podium sides with a Sun God napkin.

The men sat up, straightened their clothes and waited for Steve to announce the closing hymn.

Jane let her neighbor up, put on her clothes, and released her sons and daughters. The women held the children as they got back on the exercise bikes, treadmills and stair-steppers for the closing song.

# Chapter Seven

'We was going along the Euphrates River," says Joshua Key, a 27-year-old former U.S. soldier from Oklahoma, detailing a recurring nightmare — a scene he stumbled on shortly after the U.S. invasion of Iraq in March 2003.

"...We turned a real sharp right and all I seen was decapitated bodies. The heads laying over here and the bodies over here and U.S. troops in between them. I'm thinking, Oh my God, what in the hell happened here? What's caused this? Why in the hell did this happen? We get out and somebody was screaming, 'We fucking lost it here!' I'm thinking, Oh, yes, somebody definitely lost it here."

Joshua says he was ordered to look around for evidence of a firefight, for something to rationalize the beheaded Iraqis.

"I look around just for a few seconds and I don't see anything."

But then he noticed the sight that now triggers his nightmares.

"I see two soldiers kicking the heads around like a soccer ball. I just shut my mouth, walked back, got inside the tank, shut the door, and it was like, I can't be no part of this... Why did it happen? That's just my question: Why did that happen?"

He's convinced there was no firefight that led to the beheading orgy — there were no spent shells to indicate a battle.

"A lot of my friends stayed on the ground, looking to see if there was any shells. There was never no shells, except for what we shot. "

— Peter Laufer, <u>Mission Rejected:</u>
<u>U.S. Soldiers Who Say No to Iraq</u>

48

# Mike Palecek

On the steps of the front porch of 220 W. Angola St., two black children with glimmering skin rolled a ball made from rags and duct tape back and forth between their legs.

The boys wore only shorts, and sang a Tutsi rhyme as they pushed the ball and caught it.

They glanced up to watch young men climbing the tree in front to tap it for palm wine.

Across the street, a group of young women in saris giggled as they approached some young men wearing low-riding pants, tennis shoes without strings and bandanas.

A pride of lions yawned, sitting in the mid-day sun in the long grass of the vacant lot. Without discernible interest they watched two large elephants and one baby hustling down the dusty road following a rickshaw.

Next door a small, young, black woman minister, from the Jackson, Mississippi First Southern Baptist Church, began her service by asking those gathered to bow their heads and remember the words of Jesus.


The boys played ball on a porch almost devoid of paint, with different colors splotching here and there, as if a bunch of second graders had tired of the job on various attempts.

Monkeys played on the roof, chasing squirrels, dodging blue jays.

Graffiti on the wall of a nearby empty garage told the Eastside soldiers in Spanish to go fuck themselves.

A mural on the side of the house depicted a revolutionary leader on horseback leading peasants against tanks.

Two dogs lounged on the porch out of the sun watching the boys, their nearly closed eyes going back and forth following the ball, their tails switching at tsetse flies.

A hole the size of a boot was punched in the screen door.

Qawwali music flowed from up the block.

# The American Dream

The aroma of frybread and sage enveloped the neighborhood.

One of the dogs used his nose to pry open the screen door to go inside.

It walked over to the gold sofa, stained with a mysterious green. He hopped up and sat on the cushion, melding with the indentation perfectly.

Two identical smiling color photos of Dick hung on the wall, along with two color NASCAR race photos.

The TV was on, showing the local weatherman sweating, in his shirtsleeves, making jokes with the woman anchor that "it's going to be another warm one."

The room was dim, except for the blue glow of the television, even on this bright afternoon. The shades were pulled and the lights off.

An unopened Hamm's twelve-pack sat in the middle of the floor.

The dark gold carpet was littered as if sown with bits of potato chips.

"Be sure to sign up today for The Home Helper Show in your town," said the TV.

The dog rolled to its back, held up its paws and legs as if leaping a white picket fence, let its tongue loll out and slept, its still-active slobbery nose twitching in the direction of the stairs.

The steps ascended a narrow, shallow stairwell.

They were wooden, carelessly painted and attended by a bare, smooth, anachronistic, brand new handrail on still-shiny hangers.


The top of the stairs is not visible from the bottom. The aroma of mocha coffee reels you in.

# Mike Palecek

At the top you are completely out of breath, and you open the door because you also smell cigarettes and beer and peppermint and ink.

At first you wonder if you might have walked unannounced into the real world of Harry Potter.

There is a woman in what could be a wizard's robe, and someone sitting playing a sitar, surrounded by young people of many colors.

There is a long wooden counter.

On the counter sits a young woman with coal black hair running down her back in a long plait. She's playing air guitar and drums along with "Riding the Storm Out" coming from a CD player sitting next to her.

The rows and rows of wooden shelves are filled with books. The floors are wooden, parquet. The ceiling is a crystal clear glass dome.

There are open levels going up, up, up. On each landing people are laughing, talking, playing, reading.

You look over and down into a dimly lit bar where men and women, with suits, shorts, sandals, bare feet, turbans, stocking caps, bandanas, bald heads, ponytails, red hair, green hair, blue, are gathered around a long wooden bar.

They are wearing beards, goatees, clean-shaven faces, mustaches. They smoke American and French and Japanese and Indian cigarettes.

You walk down a few steps and squat to see that on the walls are photos: the French Resistance, Mandela on Robbin Island, Benjamin Franklin, Leonard Peltier in Leavenworth Penitentiary, Bobby Sands, Che Guevara, The Chicago Seven, Sandinistas in the jungle, Zapata on horseback, Geronimo.

You walk around the bookstore and you hear music: Indian, French, The Clash, Iranian, Argentinean, Woody Guthrie. A piercing war cry and the pounding of a drum circle sends a chill down your back.

# The American Dream

You smell incense and cookies baking and perfume and newsprint.

One wall is filled with the papers and magazines of the world.

In one darkened corner people are watching independent films using headphones, relaxing in portable cushioned chairs, drinking red and purple Slurpies and eating popcorn.

Big, lazy Saint Bernards and stray, royal cats lie around, or walk, wherever they please.

In another nook and level, folks lean way back to blast off into space in a planetarium show.

As you wander, you enter and exit the boundaries of conversations in French, English, German, Japanese, Farsi, Spanish.

You continue, still drawn along by that smell. You walk between long bookshelves toward the coffee.

At the end you see a light and smoke and people, and now you hear someone.

His tone is serious, not dramatic, but sober.

You approach and you find that you are behind the speaker, and you don't want to be, out in the open. The whole audience can see you.

Nobody notices you, but you feel uneasy, drop your eyes and find a way down the side and around to the back where you want to be.

You are standing in the back of a space with high ceiling, a square made by bookshelves.

In front a man is talking.

He is tall, thin, wearing a suit coat over an open shirt, like you imagine a college professor might. He has on jeans, brown shoes. His clothes are older maybe, but clean. You wonder why you notice those things. You realize nobody cares about that, only you.

Someone offers you coffee in a thick white mug and you think about stealing the mug.

The man is talking, standing, without a podium, without notes, and for some reason you understand this is a scheduled event.

His audience, a mixture of young and old, is seated on the floor, on mats they must have brought from home. Who brings mats to a lecture? Who *has* mats?

They are also on sofas, all manners of chairs. You catch yourself counting the colors of the stupid chairs.

They are listening. Of course.

The speaker concludes his remarks by smiling slightly and folding his hands at his waist.

"We are doomed," he says.

The crowd sits in silence and you feel embarrassed for them and the speaker.

"Mr. Otherfield?" A young girl, maybe a sixth grader, maybe fifth, wearing an actual raspberry beret, raises her hand and talks.

Why do people raise their hand if they are just going to talk right away anyway?

"Is there anything we can do?"

Otherfield shoved his hands into his pockets and tried to hide inside his shoulders.

He straightened and looked at the young girl.

"Don't forget those kids who were killed and their friends who are probably right now on their way to Gitmo.

"Most people don't care about the lies, don't want to know.

"Care.

"They want to scare you ... so that you will run to them for protection. Run away. These are the sleazy men in the cars holding out melted candy in their hands."

# The American Dream

He jerked his hands from his pockets, looked down, then up to the ceiling as he paced.

He stopped and looked again at the girl.

"Gold. Rubies. Diamonds."

He held up three fingers, stained yellow from smoking roll your own cigarettes, showing notes in ink on the palms and the back of the wrist, like homemade tattoos made in a hurry. Sanskrit? Hopi? Cuneiform?

"Why are they valuable? They have some unique functions, qualities, but we give them value way beyond that.

"And then a starving child or a homeless woman has no value. Cannot be redeemed for bus money."

He took his hand down and folded his arms over his chest.

"Find Jerry Jeff Walker." He put just his fingertips into his front pockets like a cowhand and grinned.

"High Hill Country Rain.

"I got a feeling, something that I can't explain. Like running naked in that high hill country rain," he recited.

"That means more to me than Jesus Christ himself. It's the things you find on your own that you are going to value more than the ones that get shoved in your face.

"I wish I *had* found the New Testament at a used bookstore on a rainy Saturday night, rather than getting thumped over the head with it by Father Dan for falling asleep at Mass.

"I really do."

Otherfield jerked around at the sound of a bookshelf toppling.

More shelves and chairs and statues crashed on the wood floor and a dog yelped as if it had been smashed in the head with a police woman's baton.

Otherfield and his audience dashed toward the commotion.

Outside the house, lights flashed and police cruisers, National Guard trucks and ambulances filled the neighborhood yards.

## Mike Palecek

A helicopter shined its light on the house where the twin boys lay on their sides, small bullet holes in their heads, the ball having dribbled down the grass path to the dirt road.

The dog in the front room still lay on its back, its throat sliced, blood staining the gold sofa and carpet.

National Guardsmen stomped up the stairs in hightop, shiny black boots.

The air was filled with dust and potato chips.

Upstairs in the bookstore, the stereo from the counter lay smashed on the parquet floor.

The young woman who had been playing air guitar was being mauled behind the counter by an excited group of young men in camouflage.

Smoke poured out of the lower bar level as if a grenade had gone off down there.

All around the bookstore, customers and staff members lay on the floor, arms and legs outstretched, motionless over a counter, over railings. One young man, in a rainbow colored shirt and dreadlocks, was impaled on a bayonet and stuck face-first into the one-hundred-gallon tropical fish tank.

A pretty, young, dead woman, with a garrote choking her throat, had been hauled up the flag pole in the corner, to replace the green and blue global flag.

In the middle of the wood floor policemen tossed books and magazines and newspapers into a growing fire.

In another area people sat in a circle with their hands cuffed behind their backs.

Tom Otherfield ran up to the chief of police.

"You cannot do this!" he screamed, grabbing the man's shoulders, his face red, his hair furious, his shirt untucked.

"Why are you doing this? Stop! You are insane! Stop this instant. Stop!"

# Chapter Eight

> The star-spangled banner does not fill me with
> pride: it fills me with shame, and that flag
> symbolizes sorrow and corruption to me right
> now. The flag represents so much lying, fixed
> elections, profiting by the war machine, high gas
> prices, spying on Americans, rapid erosion of our
> freedoms while BushCo literally gets away with
> murder, torture and extreme rendition,
> contaminating the world with depleted uranium,
> and illegal and immoral wars that are responsible
> for killing so many. A symbol that used to
> represent hope to so many around the world now
> fills so many with disgust.
>
> — Cindy Sheehan

There is one person in this shit hole town who understands
what is really going on here. I'm sure of that.

Somebody would have to, wouldn'tcha think?

It isn't me.

But I will tell you this, and then I've got to go mow my lawn or
something. I've tried, I quit trying — and now I wonder if it
might be time to try again.

I don't know.

I should water the tomatoes and clean my gutters.

It's like those ladies underwear pages in the Sears catalog.

Sure it is, just listen.

You're not supposed to, but everybody does, and nobody talks
about it, so you think it's not happening.

That's pretty much the story of life and you didn't have to
climb a mountain.

You can find it at Sears.

Amen.


I'm nobody.

No one you know about or have heard about or ever will. Nobody who you see at the grocery store and kind of looks familiar.

Some folks look at life through rose-colored glasses or with blinders on or through the looking glass. I look at stuff through my basement window.

I saw them take away that young man in the helicopter, and I heard a free concert in the park the next night, a Christian youth band. I opened my window just a crack and sat in the dark in my lawn chair with a glass of Tang and some ice. It was nice.

I went to prison once. It wasn't a big deal.

Not to anyone else.

To me it was a big deal.

I "did" civil disobedience and it rained just as we linked arms to walk onto the Air Force base. I sat down and cried on the other side of the fence 'cause I wasn't stupid.

I cried because I knew I was breaking up with America, and everything I had ever been I was leaving behind. I also cried because I wished I was like my friends back home, who did not even think about this stuff, who would live their lives with homes and wives and dogs and kids and shit. I was going to prison.

Oh, I knew I had to do it, it just wasn't easy. Maybe I like easy better.

I believed in America at one time, wanted very badly to be an American, a great one. I ran early morning wind sprints on my own in the summer and believed everything they told me.

# The American Dream

But it cost too much. I couldn't keep up the payments so I had to give it all back.

I did get married, had kids and worked at a job. You have to have a pretty good job to afford kids and a wife. The better your job is, the prettier wife you can afford.

And I went to prison. I don't talk about that.

For one thing, nobody ever asks; for two, it's too painful.

It's like driving down the road with a good song playing, and you start to think what it's like to have pins stuck into your eyeballs. It's easier to sing the song and look out the window at the cows and shit.

It's like that.

And we had kids. Could've had more with a better job.

Try having a family and being against America. You won't get far. They won't let you. You have to be totally on their side, or you don't get any of that shit. Health insurance, Happy Meals, gym locker, Little League. They'll take it all away in the time it takes to tell you you're not welcome anymore.

Lucky for Wheel of Fortune.

Prison.

Small town. Military. America.

Religion. High School friends. Jesus.

Parents. Girlfriend.

Poverty.

Job.

Depression.

That's about it. Life.

Take those words, students, and write your own story.

Those words have to be included or you're not done yet.

You may finish at home, but be prepared to discuss your story out loud in small groups tomorrow.

# Mike Palecek

That's it.

I don't want to tell my story.

Maybe I will. I doubt it.


Prison is hell. What a cliche.

I was in county jails and federal prisons. A few months, not years.

I'm no hero. I cried. I wanted out, wanted to go home.

But I was there.

I did it.

I did go in, "do the time" and walk out on all my release days.

I'm not a people person. You understand?

Even saying those words gives me the willies.

You pretty much are the same person in jail that you are outside except times ten.

Your qualities or lack thereof glare like 2 p.m. on a tin building.

You don't have any means of escape: go to work, go home, go for a drive, go jogging, go upstairs, go downstairs, go for a walk.

You are just you, right here, right now, all day every day — ninety days, six months, sixty years.

That's a lot.

And so I don't meet people well.

When I get called faggot I take it to heart, and pretty soon I'm too depressed to smile and the past three days look like thirty years, and I can't remember what ice cream sounds like.

There are no normal thoughts in jail.


Fence, Nebraska.

# The American Dream

Well, what it is, is a super max prison in the Sandhills of Nebraska. It was super max before super max.

Nebraska itself is a desert of the mind.

The Sandhills is a wilderness of the land.

You go to the desert, turn right and you find this little, hot, town with a pickup parked on Main Street. There is a dog in the back of the pickup, and no people in sight.

The town is called Kirby, and you take the highway headed west until all you can see are gently rolling bluffs of sand and weed clumps, no cows, no cars, no houses, nothing.

And then you take this sand road off into the sand bluffs for fourteen miles, rattling over weed clumps and sand.

Until off in the distance you see something.

The Great American Gulag in the middle of America, ranch country, where they still drive cattle, and where they rope and brand men.

Miles and miles of fence, barbed, razor, chainlink, whatever you got — constructed without a vote of Congress or even without the people in Congress knowing about it. Without a vote of the people, of course. Some presidents they didn't even tell about it.

They don't use walls, just fences, and white pickups to patrol the perimeter, and black sunglasses to protect the guards against the glare of the sun and snow.

Inside were SDS, Weather Underground, Panthers, AIM, all the revolutionaries in the United States, and a whole lot of other guys, too.

I got there on a white prison bus. Yeah, I know, I've never seen 'em either. But I know they have 'em. They kind of look like buses on their way to a pool on a hot summer day from some ghetto church.

# Mike Palecek

You know, in the prisoner population you will meet people who will say they know of prisoners who have been murdered by guards, goons, or whatever.

And before Abu Ghraib well, even being a prisoner myself, though I could see how that might be true, I still retained my doubts, still had a lot of my socialization, propagandization, Captain Kangaroozation, my thousands of hours of American TV watching, rotting inside me.

But now I know it's true.

They tortured those people in Iraq and Guantanamo because they could get away with it. Just like they do whatever, here, that they can get away with.

There is no American ideal gene.

They say we do the right thing because we are Americans.

Bullcrap.

I'll bet the German people were fed the same line about their soldiers and government and police and shit.

Anyway, we sat out in that old, crappy unmarked white bus with bars on the windows.

There's a guard in back in the shadows sweating in a cage with a gun. He's right next to the toilet, so when you have to go back and shit, with handcuffs on and shackles, you also get to have a big dumb fat guy from a used-to-be Indiana pig farm watching you, holding a short shotgun. He's eating a cheese sandwich, watching you poop. There's an American scene you didn't get read to you on a cold winter night under the clean covers.

It dawned on me, became just so obvious right then, like a revelation brought on by a storm — that the whole thing, the United States, the federal government, the walls of Leavenworth — are all made so big just to make you feel small.

Really.

# The American Dream

You wouldn't be aware of that unless you were in my shoes sitting in that window seat of that prison bus at that moment. Maybe I was lucky.

I thought of my days in Catholic school, and then training to be an altar boy after school, and how scared I was to go out with the priest as a real server my first time at morning mass before the whole school. And sister coming into the room to tell us the President had been shot, and my dad's smile when he showed me the car he had bought for me as a surprise when I turned sixteen. And how I cried because I didn't like it, instead of thanking him and hugging him and saying I appreciated how he had found the car and paid for it, and what it meant to him that I be happy.

I should have gone to prison for that, not for trying to fight lousy America.

Anyway, now me at The Fence.

Like I said, who cares?

Well I cared quite a bit.


I was having trouble with the Hispanics ever since Chicago, Terre Haute, Leavenworth, El Reno, the bus ride there. So, during the intake interview, when I was asked if there was any reason I could not go into the general prison population, I said no.

And that night I walked the small yard. The bigger one is outside, only used on weekends.

I walked by myself, big steps, strong steps, fast steps, swinging my arms, looking straight head — around and around the square — a long way from home, in the darkening Nebraska night, right up to the different Hispanic groups. I didn't say anything, just walked close by. Not staring, just being there. I just wanted to show them, I guess, that here I was if they thought something needed to happen.

It didn't. I think they didn't even notice me. But it made me feel a little better, I guess.

I made some friends in my few months there. We slept in an open dorm, which is kind of strange.

Once I wrote a letter to the unit manager, and said I wasn't going to work, in order to protest the U.S. military. I showed the letter around before I turned it in. I was also after the publicity.

They arrested me in the dorm with handcuffs in front and took me to the hole for a few days, which was interesting.

I can say interesting now. But then it was terrifying: the being alone with silence and yourself and time.

There are interesting people in federal prison.

A lot of bad people and a lot of good people.

But I wasn't there long enough to really join the fraternity of prisoners. I think. Maybe it's just my personality to feel I am always on the outside.

I don't know.

# Chapter Nine

It was for me, the world of Dick and Jane, the world
that *every* child should inhabit, a world with yellow
brick roads, the security of parental love, full
stomachs and overflowing hearts filled with warm
feelings.

— Bob Keesham, forward to
The World of Dick and Jane

On the cover of the Aug. 15, 1959 *Saturday Evening Post* is
an illustration of a young couple pitched against each other,
leaning back against a tree, dreamy gazes in their eyes as
they stare into the night sky overhead.

They see dot sketches, perhaps formed by the stars, of their
future: appliances, toasters, washers, dryers, can openers,
home, swimming pool, refrigerator with ice dispenser.

Maybe those dreams have been put there by advertising or
CIA implants or the uncle from Paducah, but it is certain they
do not realize that those are not elective items: those
modern conveniences are mandatory dreams, so to say.

For on the backside of that dream, of that dark blue night
curtain, the flip side of that 45 playing "Johnny Angel," is a
prison camp, an American prison camp, in the Midwest, with
corn on the left and soybeans on the right, a big orange
moon on a summer night with electronic eavesdropping
equipment visible on the man's nose as he stares down at a
big, sparkling red DeSoto humming down a deserted highway
with Grandma and Grandpa Jones listening to the ballgame
on the radio with their hands out the window trying to catch
the wind.

The locusts wavered and the wind died down.

The announcers signed off and the white-tailed deer stood in
the field listening.

# Mike Palecek

The red sun shined on the barn sides and the new kittens licked at the milk left in the bowl by the back door.

Tractors headed off down the lane for the fields and a UPS truck left behind a wake of dust and smoke.

It skidded to a stop to make the corner up Git Mo's lane.

They called it Git Mo's because the farm, small ranch really, once belonged to a paraplegic rancher, farmer really, name of Morris.

And when the government bought the property the name stayed since the guards were all from around here.

Not much remained of the old place.

It was more a parking lot now than a working farm or ranch that had a husband and wife and seven children running around everywhere — enough to keep the grass down without mowing.

They still had dogs, though.

There was chainlink fence and razor wire, concrete pads and long kennels topped with more razor wire.

There were guard towers.

In fact, the towers and concrete enticed more than one small airplane into landing, only to zoom back off as soon as they saw the Doberman baggage handlers.

Camp Git Mo's was divided into units, each with its own grounds, staff, rules and uniforms.

Michael M was assigned to Unit Traitor Fuck.

Among the others were Dumb Ass, Pink Boy, Wet the Bed, Faggots, Queers, Towel Heads, Sand Nigger, Corn Nigger, Jap, Gook, Kraut, Wetback, French Nigger, Retard, Coon, Disappeared, Canuck, Santiago Stadium.

M knelt on the cement run of his kennel.

# The American Dream

He wore only white panties with small red roses. His hands were tied behind his back with plastic cuffs and he wore a black hood over his head.

Inside M's kennel stood two guards, one black, one white. One was tall with large arms, the other shorter, a little thinner, maybe.

They stood on both sides of M, behind him, their hands on their hips.

Down the line of kennels M heard children's voices, not play sounds, frightened.

He then heard dogs and the gruff voices of male guards.

Then the children cried.

The dogs barked some more, and the guards shouted, and there were cracks and snaps and pops, and then the kids did not cry.

M's body was lathered in sweat. His knees were numb and his back ached and spasmed. He really, really needed to maintain his position as long as he could in order to keep from being beaten again.

Large, black speakers set just outside the kennels on the cement walking path played Toby Keith yelping at full blast.

In the kennel behind M the guards worked to arrange wires to the fingers and testicles and into the anus of a man M understood to be a baker.

A woman guard, with a tattoo of a rose on her bicep and a dolphin earring, lugged in a plastic wash tub of ice water that she placed in front of the man, who sat on a metal chair with slats through which the wires ran. He sat out on the cement run of his kennel, like somebody out enjoying the sun in America. He had a hood over his head and his white rose panties were pulled to his knees. The speaker just outside his kennel now blasted "I'm proud to be an American where at least I know I'm free" at No. 10 volume.

The man was commanded to put his feet in the water.

# Mike Palecek

"Now!"

M heard the squeals and gurgling noises and body jerks of the man each time they made him stick his feet in the water.

Then the guards started to get into it. They pelted the guy with water balloons and poured ice water over his head.

They dipped a hot dog in ketchup, attached it to the man's penis using postal rubber bands, and let three of the Dobermans into the kennel run.

M knelt in the blood from his own knees, wanting water and being afraid they would think to answer him the same way they had responded to his neighbor's request for a drink.

# Chapter Ten

We could electrify this wire with the kind of current
that would not kill, but it would be a discouragement
for them to be fooling around with it.

We do that with livestock all the time.

— Rep. Steve King [R-IA]

"The next thing I realized," said Tom Otherfield in a whisper
through his hood, "I was bouncing along in the back of a
truck. My hands and feet were bound. There were others
with me. I couldn't see them. I was blindfolded and had some
oily rag in my mouth. I couldn't hardly breathe. The fumes
made my eyes water. I thought I'd throw up and drown in my
own vomit and who would *give* a measly shit."

Otherfield knelt on the cement run of his kennel in anus and
penis blood stains from yesterday's baker barbecue.

Michael M knelt on the other side of the wire mesh. They
each faced toward the speakers outside the run, now blasting
Rush Limbaugh at them from ten feet away.

They smelled burned or burning flesh from somewhere, each
wondering how they knew what it was, and neither saying
anything to the other about it.

M repositioned his knees.

He nodded slightly to let Otherfield know he was listening.

"This country has no relation," he hissed, "would not be
recognizable to our founding fathers. There is a private army
that nobody knows about. Nobody has any control over what
they do or how much money they get. They do what they
want, whenever they want. And forty percent of the military
budget is secret."

He paused to lower his head to his chest to cough.

"Who made that rule? It's funny. Goddamn hilarious. Geezuz!"

Otherfield paused and M thought it might be his turn to talk.

"I need to be on The Home Helper Show," he said, in a hiss.

"The what?"

"That show where they come in and fix up your home. It's on TV."

"Oh. Yeah, I've heard of it. You're going to be on it? When? I'd like to watch."

"No, no, I have to register first. I'm not *registered*," M whispered. "First you have to be registered."

Otherfield asked how you get registered.

"Just send it in. I have to get word to my wife," he hissed, "to get us registered."

"Of course," said Otherfield.

A guard walked by in heavy boots, making sure to scuff his heels on the cement so that the prisoners would know he was coming, so they would stop talking, so that he would not have to work overtime — it was almost the end of his shift — to discipline them. He wanted to get home to take his kids to the park.

"Money," Otherfield whispered hoarsely.

"What?" said M.

"Lies, military, to hell with the poor, bombs, bombs, and then call it all Christian. Wow.

"You know ..."

"Huh?"

I said, "You know?"

"You get more news right here, by taking a walk in the dark, by starting a conversation with a man surrounded by pigeons, than you do by reading the *New York Times*."

"The what?"

"And all the while the people in the neighborhoods wake up and go to sleep dreaming of a new kitchen."

# The American Dream

"Swimming pool," said M.

"What?" said Otherfield.

"And kitchen." M put his face right in the sun to try to see anything through his black hood.

"The people in charge couldn't dream up a better deal than that," said Otherfield.

"Sshh!" said the guard on his way back. "Shut the fuck up," he hissed.

"What?" said M. "What'd he *say*?"

# Chapter Eleven

When we were doing the night raids in the houses,
we would pull people out and have them all on their
knees and zip-tied. We would ask the man of the
house questions. If he didn't answer the way we
liked, we would shoot his youngest kid in the head.
We would keep going, this was our interrogation. He
could be innocent. He could be just an average Joe
trying to support his family. If he didn't give us a
satisfactory answer, we'd start killing off his family
until he told us something. If he didn't know anything,
I guess he was SOL.

> — Jessie Macbeth, former Army Ranger
> and Iraq war veteran

I was telling you about prisons, part of my essay, remember?

And the rest of that list, well, I know for a fact.

You don't want to hear my life story and I don't want to hear
yours.

If I get on "Wheel of Fortune" or "Survivor" or "Screw Your
Sister," then you'll want to know all about me.

But not now.

I'll say one little bit about each of them and that's it. If you
don't like it, screw it, and screw you, too.

Nah, on second thought, get outa here. You ain't about
nothin'.

Go on.

Go.

# Chapter Twelve

We came to fight the Jihad
And our hearts were pure and strong
As death filled the air, we all offered up our prayers
And prepared for our martyrdom
But Allah had some other plan,
Some secret not revealed
Now they're draggin' me back
With my head in a sack
To the land of the infidel.

— Steve Earl, "John Walker's Blues"

On the green, chipped tables outside the Homeland City Pool, fat people sat licking ice cream cones and wiggling their toes to get rid of the little red ants.

A woman and a man were on one side of one table.

She wore a two-piece cherry red suit, with bits of hair like cactus poking out between her legs.

The man wore jean shorts with the ends frizzled. His knees were red.

The "lunch area" slumped outside the chainlink fence around the square pool — two picnic tables outside the snack bar, which was part of the pool building complex that also included changing rooms and bathrooms and showers.

The lifeguard blasted her whistle at someone taking too many warm-ups on the diving board.

A droplet of sweet sweat formed on the forehead of the woman. It sat there, stuck for a moment in a crevice.

The pool was full of splashing and open mouths, like a trout farm tourist trap on the highway.

A very similar droplet formed on the forehead of the man.

He breathed deep to catch his breath.

## Mike Palecek

The lifeguard blasted her whistle again to signify break time, everybody out.

The man and woman looked at each other and then at their children.

The droplets of sweat grew ever larger as the sun settled into two o'clock. No clouds were visible in the light blue. Both beads of perspiration began to move, heading intuitively for the nose passageway.

Both man and woman began to breathe heavily. They looked at each other. The woman licked sweat from her upper lip with a cow tongue.

The ball of salt water on the woman's nose skidded down, flew off the nose and slid over her sumptuous closed, chewing mouth. She stared out over the parking lot like a Holstein on afternoon break.

She ran her red tongue out long and licked the runny, melting, spent ice cream cone, keeping the bottom from dripping onto her gigantic, powerful thighs. She looked over at her man, and adjusted a strap on her suit by repositioning her bottom on the flaking bench.

In the meantime, his sweat pustule leaped from his nose to his belly and held tight to a clump of hair, peering down into the black hole in the belly. He wheezed, coughed and tried not to stop breathing.

Her sweat found its way down and around her chin, whooshed playfully over the moguls and down her neck, where it rolled and rocked like a small boat in an ocean storm, ending up on her bosom where it stared down into the darkness.

He looked at her and she at him, letting their accumulated sweat fall over their breasts and balls and leg rash and hairy vagina.

They breathed deeply and stared at each other, mouths partially open for air, like carp left on the bank on purpose.

# The American Dream

The lifeguard blew her whistle signaling that break time was over.

The woman opened her lips wide, let loose her longing, lapping, wet tongue, welcoming in the rest of her dripping, soppy, saggy, lifeless cone.

She chewed once and swallowed.

The man snorted and coughed and bent over to spit.

He grabbed his knees and looked as if he might vomit, then sat straight to wipe his face with the back of his hand.

The two got up to go back into the pool area as the children wiped their sticky fingers on the grass.

# Chapter Thirteen

Although it is not true that all conservatives are
stupid people, it is true that most stupid people are
conservative.

— John Stuart Mill

This is John, from the underground, looking out at you from
some basement window of a house in Homeland. It's not a
home without children, without someone to share it with.
Just a house.

They call me John the Baptist because they've seen me
micturating on the flowers around town at night.

I can't stand you, the sight of you, the thought of you, the
very concept of you.

If I had a remote control of my own, and I saw your fucking
ass driving down the road at five miles an hour without
another moving vehicle in sight, I'd point and click and blow
your careful ass to holy hell.

How's it going?

Hot enough for ya?

Goddamn right I would.

There are those in America who knew that this was not the
land of the free and the home of the brave long before Abu
Ghraib. Those people are the poor, the prisoner, the activist,
the immigrant. Anyone who has found himself face to face
with the real, ugly face of America: the judge, the guard, the
policeman, the soldier.

You know, though, you can make most people believe
anything.

# The American Dream

They'll swallow the Star Spangled Banner with their Wheaties;
they will believe they'll burn in hell for eating fish on Friday or
not entering the building on the corner at least once every
Sunday. Tell 'em there's this place called Purgatory and tell
them they live in a democracy and that everyone in a crowd
of rich people in Washington, D.C. has their very own
personal best interests on index cards taped to their
bathroom mirrors.

And tell them we went to the moon once and never went
back, and that the CIA works for them and the peace dividend
when Russia folded, well, just didn't quite work out, but we
tried.

Tell 'em the war on drugs is vital to their lives, too, while
you're at it, and then make sure you get the rugs out of the
closet for nap time at ten.

You can tell them a million and one things; they will believe it.

In America there isn't one born every minute, more like every
second or something, more like that.

Those were drone airplanes that hit those towers and the
real ones are at the bottom of the ocean. Where's my CBS
Christmas Special?

Will the American people ever wake up? I wonder. I don't
think so, really.

Even the poor Americans have their flags waving from the
coat hanger antenna duct-taped to the side of the trailer.

Well, if there was any amount of real religion spoken in any of
these jillion churches, and if the newspaper reporters actually
wanted to find something out, the lies and the rich and the
corrupt couldn't stand up to that tidal wave.

But the churches and the reporters are just a dribble, no
more'n I leak on myself after I think I'm done peeing in the
war memorial flowers after dark.

Back in the 1960s we really thought things were possible:
civil rights, stop war, war on poverty — what else ya got?
Bring it on, motherfucker.

But somebody got smart and killed Martin and the Kennedys and that was that.

Have you seen the photos of all those black people lining the tracks when Bobby's body was brought back? That meant something. Those folks felt something and just standing there said it.

Now it's more like nothing is possible. It is. Stop war? Stop poverty? Free the prisoners? Woodstock Nation?

You *got* to be kidding me, fool.

I go to work at seven and mow the lawn when I get home. When do I got time to stop poverty?

Okay. Terre Haute. Lincoln. Council Bluffs. Omaha. Underground.

Yes, I was underground, in the parlance of the 1960s. You didn't know that, did you? You didn't care. I know.

The Weather Underground, SDS, those guys. Black Panthers, on CBS News, blowing up buildings in Madison, Wisconsin, getting murdered by FBI pre-dawn raids.

That wasn't me.

Nah.

But I heard about it.

I got locked in my grandparents' basement.

But blowing things up, blowing people up. I've thought about it. I've thought about Ghandi and Berrigan and I've also thought about Jesus and Che and Castro and the Sandinistas and Sitting Bull and Paul Revere.

I wonder what Paul Revere did after he woke everybody up. I wonder if that was a fast horse he was on. Did he go back and shoot and get shot? Or maybe he walked down the middle of the road with his hands held up asking everybody not to kill each other. Or maybe he just kept going.

I dunno.

# The American Dream

Well, when I was a senior in high school, I found some warm Schlitz in my grandfather's downstairs woodshop, turned up the radio and drank it. It got dark and I couldn't find my way to the door. They were gone over to somebody's house.

I sat there. On their dirt floor, under the canned goods, listening to Chopin and then the Cardinals game and I didn't think about Castro or Ghandi the whole night. I just dreamed in the dark about Mary Kleinsasser and wondered what my parents were going to say in the morning.

When I woke up I found the door and walked outside in about thirty seconds. Then I took an hour to walk home and I told my Dad all about Che and the Black Panthers and how I was hiding out from the government, all night long.

He just looked at me.

He could probably still smell the beer.

Then I went to jail, went crazy, went home.

That's about it.

I was going to tell you now about jail, as if you fucking cared, motherfucker.

That's gonna have to wait. It's time for me to water the zinnias.

# Chapter Fourteen

I was eight years old when President John Kennedy
was shot to death in Dallas in 1963. If grace favors
me, I'll be 62 when documents related to the
assassination are released to the public, and 84
when the Warren Commission's investigative files
into the tragedy are finally opened.

That's a long time to wait for a chance to evaluate
the purported truth.

It's a blot on the presumed sophistication of the
people of the United States that any aspect of an
event so dramatic and shocking should be kept from
us. Perhaps it's true, to abuse the line from *A Few
Good Men* yet again, that we can't handle the truth.
But there cannot be genuine resolution as long as
such critical information remains concealed.

— Robert Steinback, *Boston Globe*

Omaha. Lincoln. Council Bluffs.

I've spent considerable time in those county jails, nothing that
would win any county fair prizes, but plenty enough to my way
of thinking.

All for trying to topple the American empire.

I would, too.

If I could I'd tie a rope around the Statue of Liberty and pull
her into whatever bay or river that is. And then ram a
flagpole way up her ass and call her Barbara Bush.

If I could will it, every little explosion in my toilet when I push
that silver knob would mean an American military base in
Alabama, or a little bullet factory in Iowa, or some fucking
high school history propaganda classroom in Indiana is blown
to kingdom come.

# The American Dream

I wouldn't have even thought about that if I hadn't ever gone to jail.

It's the way you think now.

You are a tourist.

You haven't really been to the United States.

You flit around and take pictures of all the tinsel and bows.

I've walked down the side streets.

Yep. Mt. Rushmore, come tumblin' down.

Glory.

Hallelujah.

And I do believe ol' Jesus would put a hand on the rope along with me. Yes'm he would.


Well, I like jail with bars more than windows. With the bars they are being honest. This is jail.

With the windows they are saying this is human, we care about you. That's one of the biggest lies there is going.

I don't care what food they serve. It's all good to me. Lots complain about that, but it's no thing with me.

Boredom is the most frightening thing there is.

You don't even know it and you develop a prisoner's look.

You look at yourself in the car mirror and you don't recognize yourself. If that's how your face looks, wonder what your insides are like.

After you get out it's very hard to be around people.

It's like you fight to get a real breath on this planet. You cannot live in this atmosphere.

They talk and laugh about things that make you want to take the heel of your hand and ram their noses back through their skulls. It could be the price of gas or the best route through a road construction zone. You wish they were dead. More than dead. Destroyed.

Jesus would never run a jail. I know that.

And he'd never pay for one or vote for one or lay block for one.

He'd be inside, crying, sweating, shivering, being scared, depressed. He'd have a rash running from his palms up both arms, and wondering if they really do stab people at dinner time, and why do the guards do this sort of work. And is he really a homo? He didn't think he was a homo. Maybe he is a homo. He *must* be a homo.

Oh, God. How can I kill myself?

I have no right to live.

He'd sit in the visiting room trying to get the words out.

I ... can't ... do ... this ... anymore.

And no sound, he could not talk.

That's what would Jesus do.

Terre Haute is a red brick penitentiary, as I recall, in what is supposed to be the goodest of the good ol' USA, Indiana. Which gives you one clue.

It's big and it will kill you.

They do not care about forgive your neighbor and thou shall not kill or that your young son is sitting home looking out the front window for his Dad to read to him.

They don't care about none of that and that's another clue about what is America.

I stayed in Terre Haute in a barred cage, in a long run of cells, for about three weeks.

I had to walk down the run to the phone to talk to my wife once a week, and while I'm trying not to die of depression right there and asking her how work is and how her mom is, I've got guys three feet behind me saying things about me you don't want to hear, and then I walk back for another week's worth.

# The American Dream

I masturbated and thought about killing myself and scribbled Eagles lyrics on the wall. I imagined mice running around my cell, and voices, and I wished I could be playing ball in the backyard or face-down dead.

I was in prison for trying to stop war and giving the war money to the poor. When I prayed that's what ol' Jesus told me. If there is a Jesus. I still think there is.

So I did it.

And that's why these poor people in prison are saying they want to fuck me. Oh, well, who cares.

I guess I'd do it again, if I had to.

I'm not going to join no peacenik demonstration, even though I still agree with them. I'm just not volunteering for jail this time, let's just say that. This time there's gonna be a fight. If there is a this time, which I doubt. I just know I'm no damn Ghandi. Ghandi's fine and all that. But he ain't me and I ain't him. I found that out sure enough.

Shit.

If that's not doing enough, then so be it. They can come get me. They know where to look. The peaceniks *and* the *po*lice.

Geezuz, when is this fucking essay going to be over?

Was I cowardly? A liar? Homosexual? Not a hero? Wrong?

Ohhh, Jesus.

Take out the new steak knife set and bring it upstairs when everyone is gone and cut, cut, cut. Pull up the worst thoughts and let them run through my veins. What hurts the most?

Stick it. Stick it.

My Dad.

He smiled so wide when I walked in the back door after hitchhiking from Oregon.

"He's here!" he hollered. That sent shivers down my back.

I always wanted to just tell him to his face that I loved him. I think he did, too.

We shook hands when I left for college, and he tried to engage me each time I came home for the weekend with a word game series the paper was running. That was a valiant effort, and I also tried to make it work. We failed, just like lots of dads and sons, I imagine.

When he died I cried like there was no tomorrow. I had never seen a real death rattle before. I threw things around his hospital room. We were leaving the hospital and I told Mom, just one minute. I took the elevator back to his room and he was alone. I went in and heard breathing. He's alive! And it was just his oxygen tube still on.

Mom and I were driving home from Omaha and I told her that right now Dad was meeting Jesus, which was very cool to imagine, comforting. I hope it really happened. He was a good guy.

Friends, parents. Oh, shit, you can wait. Go watch TV or bake a Pillsbury cake or some shit.

Wait.

There was this one guy in Terre Haute. A young, little tough guy.

He was from I forget.

He gave me his cigarettes as he was leaving, headed for Con Air or a bus or something.

He said, "I like somebody with heart."

Wow.

Now, that meant something.

A stadium full of big-hair ministers screaming Jesus make it rain tootsie rolls don't mean scat compared to that.

Wow. Wow.

All right.

Please, go away.

# Chapter Fifteen

There was one exact moment, in fact, when I knew for sure that Al Gore would never be President of the United States, no matter what the experts were saying — and that was when the whole Bush family suddenly appeared on TV and openly scoffed at the idea of Gore winning Florida. It was nonsense, said the candidate, utter nonsense ... Anybody who believed Bush had lost Florida was a fool. The media, all of them, were liars and dunces and treacherous whores trying to sabotage his victory ... Here was the whole bloody family laughing and hooting and sneering at the dumbness of the whole world on national TV. The old man was the real tip-off. The leer on his face was almost frightening. It was like looking into the eyes of a tall hyena with a living sheep in its mouth. The sheep's fate was sealed, and so was Al Gore's.

> — Hunter S. Thompson,
> ESPN, Nov. 27, 2000

They call me "Butterfly".

Not.

It's not that. I probably weigh as much as a million butterflies. Or more, probably, I don't know.

It's because when I knocked Jim down in the lunchroom for calling me a pig, I stood over him and yelled at him to get up so I could knock him down again.

He wouldn't. He's not as stupid as he looks, I guess.

Sanndra said I looked like Muhammed Ali on the History Channel.

They also call me "Rosey The Riveter".

It's like that one pretty young woman on the poster with her sleeves rolled up showing her muscle, saying something like we can handle it or something. It was for one of the wars. Well, there's a WWF wrestler called Rosey The Riveter, too, so we were watching and Sanndra says I look like her.

Sanndra calls me that, too. Maybe she watches too much TV.

Rosey The Riveter, the Butterfly.

Whatever. Ain't no thang.

My dog is worried.

That worries me.

Tuffy's my dog but he's at my parents'. I see him when I go there and he looks worried, about something.

People.

You can't live with 'em and you can't live with 'em.

I guess I thought the sit-down protest was pretty neat and most everybody else does too.

Sometimes now when staff tells us we're having hamburger helper or we have to work a Saturday morning to get caught up we say we're going to have a sit-down protest.

And they have to pay attention 'cause they know we could. That's pretty cool.

I think we should have a sit-down protest about what's going on in Homeland.

They're not nice.

Most people are nice to disabled people. I'm disabled. Some aren't. Some stare, but they probably don't know they are.

But nobody is nice to Mexicans or poor people.

They think there's something wrong or bad about them. Something they should be afraid of, something about those people.

# The American Dream

They're not afraid of us. We embarrass or annoy some people, but let me tell you, absolutely nobody is afraid of us. I'm a hundred percent sure.

I read this column, "HomeTown", in the Homeland newspaper, by this white-haired lady that looks like Aunt Bee. There's recipes for jello and soup and she was asking would today's youth follow Hitler. Well, of course they would, and they do and they are, today, this morning, tonight.

They follow anyone, like puppies, and you train them to hunt and kill as they grow.

She said Hitler was not a Christian. Actually, he was. The Nazi fighter planes had "Got Mitt Us" on the side. God is with us. My dad said.

And, in Hitler's Germany in 1939, Aunt Bee would write "HomeTown" in her little town's newspaper and give recipes, asking would today's good Hitler youth have followed Napoleon.

I go to church. I help with the wheelchairs and sit in the first row and I don't understand.

I don't know what they're talking about fighting evil.

Makes me think of a little Mexican kid with horns.

We moved here for a funeral. We came here from Kentucky, my folks and me, and we just stayed.

That was quite a long time ago.

# Chapter Sixteen

"I would like to thank Providence and the Almighty for choosing me of all people to be allowed to wage this battle ..."

— Adolph Hitler

"I trust God speaks through me. Without that, I couldn't do my job."

— George W. Bush

The home business sign in the front flowers said **United We Tanned**. The one-story brick ranch style home was at 2199 Hedgeview, on the corner. Election signs decorated the massive green lawns of each of the homes down the street:

**Run Dick**
**See Dick Run**
**Dick & Jane**
**Dick, Jane & Spot**
**Go Dick**

On the corner a cross made of dozens of popsicle sticks stood by the fire hydrant. It was draped with many colored hair bows. A color photo of a happy child in a pretty white dress sat on the ground. The memorial commemorated the time the doctor's little girl had crashed her tricycle and skinned her knees.

Set in each window of every home was a Neighborhood Bogeyman Watch Area poster, with one big eye, warning:

## We Are Watching You!

| | | |
|---|---|---|
| **Liberals** | **Democrats** | **Greens** |
| **Dougs** | **Mexicans** | **Negroes** |
| **Russians** | **Albanians** | **Californians** |
| **Dandelions** | **Anyone on Foot** | **Sand Niggers** |
| **Dragons** | **Snakes** | **Dinosaurs** |
| **Alligators** | | **Crocodiles** |
| **Mosquitoes** | **Ticks** | **Ants** |

# The American Dream

All the Heavens were welcomed on the curb by their hosts and the other guests.

The dozen or so folks were drenched in sweat, as if they had spent the afternoon pelting each other with water balloons. The private fund-raising, grill-out party for Dick's re-election was one of several that Dick and Jane would have to endure that evening.

The group moved around to the back, admiring the grass on the way.

Everyone on the patio moved to one side to allow Dick one-half of the area. All except Dick and Jane held Freedom Fizz drinks in clear plastic cups. Many of them looked out of one eye at the golfers, on the course just beyond the back yard, and out of the other to see if Dick had begun to speak.

"Nay-sayers," said Dick, and everyone formed a semi-circle around him. Sweat sat on their forearms as on the walls of an underground cave.

"Mumbo-jumbo."

Dick held up his personal cup — a bright yellow with a color photo of he and Jane and Spot, with their names below in red and blue and green — to punctuate, and everyone tittered and nodded.

"4-11.

"A free people."

Dick took a drink and watched someone tee-off on Number Nine.

"Has anyone read the Warren Commission report? 9/11 Truth Commission report? Patriot Act?"

Everyone shook their heads.

"The Bill of Rights? Grapes of Wrath?

"Of course not!

"We have lives! God-given lawns! We love life! We love the Sun God and he loves us! 411! May the Sun God bless Homeland."

Dick raised his head directly to the sun and closed his eyes tight, then put his head down. Everyone else closed their eyes and dipped their chins to their chests.

"They hate our buns of steel," said Dick with eyes clamped tight, lips clenched. His audience nodded as one, a few began to cry.

"You hear incredible rural legends," said Dick with a sweat droplet building on his nose, "about how illegal aliens, UFOs, did not fly into our beloved elevator. Four-one-one. Get a clue.

"How we do not need to continue with research into the retractable dome to protect us against illegal aliens? And you wonder how these people function, how they carry on normal lives.

"Well, they don't. Thank the Sun God for that, praise Him, praise his holy name."

He raised his head and his cup and reached out to click with each person in the group.

Then Dick set his cup on a white metal table and took off running around the home.

The "home run trot" had become Dick's cornerstone policy initiative.

The people applauded as he left and continued to clap until he appeared lathered in sweat around the opposite corner of the house, hands up around his armpits, pumping straight back and forth, licking sweat from his upper lip.

# Chapter Seventeen

One of the wilder stories circulating about Sept. 11,
and one that has attracted something of a cult
following among conspiracy buffs is that it was
carried out by 19 fanatical Arab hijackers,
masterminded by an evil genius named Osama bin
Laden, with no apparent motivation than that they
'hate our freedoms'.

— Gerard Holmgren

M knelt on the concrete of his kennel run. Through his black
hood he could feel the sun and the cloudless sky.

He wondered if his wife and kids were at the park.

He knelt with back straight and hands tight with plastic cuffs
behind his back.

Warm piss flowed through his white, rose-patterned panties
onto his leg, to the cement. He tried to rub it away with his
knee.

He could hear them bringing Otherfield out. He was talking
again, or still.

T.O. always babbled, though it was not allowed. They hit him
in the stomach with the black bats, then on the back, the
neck, the legs, the feet.

Still he ran on.

He was either trying to make them believe he was crazy, or
he was crazy, or he was one strong son of a bitch. The
guards did not hit him so much anymore, no matter how
much he talked.

Some even spoke with Otherfield, gave him cigarettes and let
him pull up his hood to smoke.

"If you can keep it ... thanks, man."

# Mike Palecek

Otherfield flexed his hands and pulled his hood up to his forehead to puff on his Marlboro Light.

"A republic, if you ...you got one more for my man here, Captain M, Commander Marvelous, Mr. Mike? Huh, dude?"

The guard hesitated, looked around, then stuck a cigarette through the chain link.

"M, stand up," said Otherfield.

M continued to kneel.

"Dude, he can't see," said Otherfield.

"Stand," said the guard.

M struggled to stand.

"Turn around, back up."

M turned, and fell back against the fence. The guard cut his handcuffs with a box cutter and put a lit cigarette into his hand.

"Kneel," said Tom.

M knelt and pulled up his hood.

They smoked while the guard walked to the end of the run, right up to the speaker blasting a garbled mess of Paul Harvey, Robert Schuller and Tom Brokaw.

Tom shuffled on his knees over to the end of his run, closer to M, who was light-headed from the cigarette.

"Schools," Otherfield hissed, "science classes, colleges, MIT, lunches, dinners ..."

"What?" M pinched his eyes against the smoke.

"Tassels, gowns, promising grad students, older teachers, nine times a day, all summer, fucking, on the commons lawn ..."

"What?"

"Yet they don't question how the grain elevator came straight down, at the speed of something being dropped from that height. No resistance, no pauses, no bending."

# The American Dream

"What?"

"Katie Couric is sucking on the cock of the president of CBS before she goes on camera — got it in both hands — says 'Looks good to me.' Ooh, aah, slurp, swallow. 'Looks good to me.'"

"Really?"

"That guy running against Dick Heavens?" Otherfield continued, flicking his butt through the wire toward the guard's walk. "A *Car Talk* liberal. Rattles on about lawn watering and no fat kindergarten teachers. Those are important issues, but nothing about the Westside, war, poverty or killing. Worthless cardboard piece of crap."

"What?"

"You need to get out of here."

"Really?"

"To get registered."

# Chapter Eighteen

Little Bush says we are at war, but we are not at
war because to be at war Congress has to vote for
it. He says we are at war on terror, but that is a
metaphor, though I doubt if he knows what that
means. It's like having a war on dandruff, it's endless
and pointless. We are in a dictatorship that has
been totally militarized, everyone is spied on by the
government itself. All three arms of the government
are in the hands of this junta.

— Gore Vidal

On Thursday afternoon a couple sat on their front porch
rocking, enjoying the sun, holding paper plates to their brows
against the glare.

On the sidewalk a young boy wearing a red and blue Twins
ballcap turned backward balanced on a skate board, headed
downhill.

Around the corner a cat scampered across the street
headed for the shade. It paused in the middle to scratch and
sniff a flat robin.

Two NASCAR flags, No. 8 and No. 3, stuck out from the
white front porches on opposite sides of the street, like hard-
ons of two Down's Syndrome kids on the playground.

A green leaf fluttered straight down.

In the front window of The Cafe a group of older men in
colored seed corn caps sipped coffee with old hands
overmatching the dainty cups.

A man held on as he rode a green mower, swathing back and
forth over the side lawn of the Reformed Church. Blue Jay
calls pierced the air at long intervals, like boat horns in a fog
of dense boredom.

# The American Dream

Two young mother walkers hustled along, pumping arms, smiling at every opportunity. Two shirtless college summer workers, from the construction crew at the high school gymnasium project, paused to watch, hands on hips.

A group of kids sat in the middle of the concrete basketball court at the park, with the ball in the middle of the circle.

A young man locked the door of the closed Mexican grocery store, wiped his brow and got on his daughter's pink bicycle to head home. Without noticing, he passed a series of Burma-Shave style road signs in black and white:

**Boo!**
**Be Afraid**
**Stay Awake**
**Stay Alert**

On the edge of town, a driver looked left to notice, on a small dairy farm, all the cows grouped together to look in the window. Behind them, in the brome grass of the ditch, the farmer and wife also faced the house, looking in at the cows and the bedroom and the painting on the wall — and the painting is the same scene, the room, the cows in the yard, the couple in the ditch.


M knelt in his run. Otherfield asked him if he still needed to get registered.

"Yeah."

"A new pool would be great," said Otherfield.

"I know."

"Why don't you go?"

"Go?"

"Get registered."

"Get registered. Like how?"

"Ask the guards."

"Ask them what?"

"If you can go. Tell them you need to get registered for a new pool and to be on television."

"Fuck you."

"Fuck me? No, really."

"Yeah, right."

Otherfield shuffled over on his knees. "Offer them something. They are not unreasonable."

"Aaah!"

The cries of someone in another kennel grouping caused M to go rigid involuntarily. "Offer?"

"They like candy," said Otherfield, "and baubles, trinkets."

"Trinkets? Baubles?" M thought.

He put his chin to his chest to look down his hood at his putty white doughy stomach and his rose panties and scabbed knees.

"They like gold," said Otherfield, "gold teeth, gold fillings."

"I didn't need to hear that," said M.

At four-thirty a guard brought two pans into M's run and placed them on the cement. One was filled to the brim with warm water. The other had a mush not unlike soggy dog food.

The guard pulled M's hood up so that he could lean over to eat, careful as always not to fall in face-first.

When M had finished his meal, the guard took him under the arm to pull him to his feet and walk him to his cage. When the guard let him in, M crawled to his bed, the box being too short to allow him to stand.

M now slept on a wire mattress without handcuffs or hood. There was a five-gallon bucket for his restroom, and a wash rag that was dipped into cold water once in awhile, then set back into the cage so that he could freshen up.

# The American Dream

As M lay on his back in the darkness of his wooden box, its criss-cross pattern formed in his back and arms and legs. Outside he could hear the speakers repeating the sound of an AM radio dial being continually changed. He heard shouting as he did every night, plus screams, cries, groans and barking.

M thought of his children, the way the four-year-old giggled when you pushed him on the swing and how the two-year-old walked into the kitchen in the morning with her footy pajamas, clutching her Baby Doll. He tried to remember his wife's face, but got only her hair, her body and her hands, the way she liked to keep her fingernails long and different colors.

He lay there, and maybe he fell asleep.

Then he heard a dog bark, and an owl hoot in response.

M heard bootsteps on cement, and keys. The door opened outward, tossing the light from the tower onto the box floor.

A guard threw down a pile of clothes.

"Go 'head."

M crawled up slowly and tentatively put on his T-shirt, socks, tennis shoes and jeans, with small tears and bloodstains from the crash into the war memorial.

"What is happening?" M asked.

The guard shined a flashlight into his own hand and showed two gold teeth, an opened pack of Juicy Fruit gum and three buttons, one red, one green, one silver.

"You are free to go," said another guard, outside the door.


M let one guard escort him out of Unit Traitor Fuck and past some of the others — Dumb Ass, Dune Coon, Kremlin's Kids.

He heard dogs barking and whining.

The full moon showed the guard towers, razor wire and box latrines in an elegant light.

# Mike Palecek

The guard, rifle slung over his shoulder, walked with M along the long dirt lane to the mailbox in the shape of a tractor. He nodded down the road and turned to walk slowly back, kicking up dirt with a purpose on each left-foot stride.

M gazed back at the prison camp, at the light still on in the warden's living room, at how the smoke from the guard quarters rose straight up and the big flag at the checkpoint hung limp — no wind. He sighed, turned toward the road and began walking, scuffling, kicking at rocks and rifts.

He began to hum, then sing, "and I'll gladly stand right next to you and defend her, hmm, mmm, mmm."

M kept walking down the side of the graveled country road. He wondered how far he was from Homeland, or anywhere. He recalled all the towns and fields and the smells of pigs and cows they had flown over to get here. He wondered if he could walk that far back.

"Prob'ly not," he said out loud.

M stopped and turned in a circle. He looked up and dropped his mouth open to look at all the stars. He stared at the moon, and thought he saw the American flag.

He kept gazing, catching himself from falling backward. He turned his head slightly and tried looking at the moon at an angle, with peripheral vision. He tried holding one hand over one eye, then the other eye, and then resumed walking.

M passed shadows of cows.

A deer stopped in front of him, turned guardant, then flagged its tail to bound into the ditch and over the fence.

M began to see better. He stopped at the mouth of a short farm lane and looked inside the house.

He could see the stocking feet of a man with the footrest of his recliner up. In his hand was the clicker, pointed at the TV. On the screen was The Home Helper Show.

M looked up and down the road, and hustled over to a wide tree to peek around.

# The American Dream

On the television he saw the handsome young construction crew leaning on shovels, taking a break from the digging of a swimming pool in some lucky family's backyard. They gathered together for a sideways group hug, waving to the camera.

M sighed.

He thought, if he could walk up to the house and ask the man if he could call his wife or borrow a stamp, and get registered for the Homeland Home Helper Show, then he could just walk home or whatever.

He stepped around the tree, tiptoeing, his heart pumping full blast. A dog barked somewhere near the house.

The man lifted and turned in the chair, and strained to see what was happening outside. M was just ten feet from the man in the white T-shirt looking out the big side picture window in the white farm house.

M stopped. He held his breath and opened his eyes and mouth as wide as possible. He put his hands flat against his cheeks.

"Aaaah!" he screamed.

The man in the chair fought the lever to get down and look out the window at an angle where he could see something.

"Aliens!" M screamed. "Infidels!"

And he ran.

"Jew Dogs!

"Fucking Homos!

"Gooks!

"Spearchuckers!

"Injuns!

"Towel heads! Jungle bunnies! Pollocks! Micks! Puerto Ricans!

"Commies!

"Liberals! Democrats! Fat people! Mexicans!"

# Mike Palecek

"Aaah! They are here, living among us!"

He sprinted out of the yard and through the ditch and down the road a mile or more, at least until he could not see the house. He ran and he screamed and his chest ached and his thighs burned.

"Illegal people!" he coughed.

"Somebody, help!

"Somebody! Call Rotary, find a notary." He stopped, out of breath, hands on hips, face upturned toward the sky, trying to catch a breath.

The dog woofed and ran to the edge of the yard, then trotted back, wagging its tail to greet the man in the white T-shirt, who had come outside in stocking feet to see what was going on.

M continued to run, shouting, not unlike Paul Revere, trying to warn the people that their freedom was in imminent peril.

Out of breath again, he skidded to a stop. He grabbed his knees. He saw headlights coming down the road. He made himself climb into the ditch, then up to the barbed wire fence. He hurried, struggled to fit between the strands, catching his shirt somewhere.

The lights were gliding closer. They seemed higher and brighter than a human vehicle thing, and an ominous shade. M reached behind to his back to find where his shirt was caught.

He fumbled and cursed and tore himself free, then fell in a heap into two soft cow things.

His hands pressed into the piles as if he were doing a pushup.

Through the wire and the grass M gaped as he held his breath and turned his head to watch the lights float by on the road.

Then he heard the crunching gravel as a PitchBlack Chevy Blow Job hummed past with the windows open and the sun roof pitched to the moon, and inside a CD blaring "I'm proud to be an American" ...

"Where at least I know I'm free," M sang along.

He put down a knee to free a hand to swipe a tear. He smelled the gravel smoke, then stood to wipe his hands on his shirt and pants. He stumbled through the coarse grass and weeds to sit against a thick, rough tree.

He set his head against the bark and let his arms drop to his sides at the same time that he stretched his legs out as far as they would reach. "See the USA, in a Chevrolet."

M closed his eyes for a moment and let out a long sigh, then opened them and enjoyed the full moon and the stars.

"Can't forget the men who died," he sang in a low tone to himself, "and gave this life to me."

M looked for the Sky God flag on the moon, and there it was again, just where his father had told him it was, above the corner of the mouth, on the right side, like a beauty mark.

M wondered if the man in the moon was gay, but then agreed with himself that could not be true.

"It's more like a mole," he said out loud.

The stars blinked like they did on the opening promo for "Bewitched."

"Flintstones, meet the Flintstones," M sang.

"In the town of Bedrock. It's a place right out of his-to-ry.

"Have a yabba dabba do time, a dabba do time, you'll have a hmm ol' time!"

M let his eyes close.

He opened them.

The land was lit.

The sun was not in sight.

M looked for the guards and listened for the breakfast pans.

# Mike Palecek

He heard a dog bark and went rigid. He winced and turned his head away from the sound. His hands became fists and his toes curled. His butt muscles balled and his neck muscles constricted. His jaw clenched.

M remembered the night and looked around for the Shiny Black Blow Job.

He groaned and moved his legs, brought his knees to his chest, and wrapped his arms around them.

He sucked a deep breath, smiled and sang to himself softly, "The best part of waking up ... is Folgers in your cup."

A rooster crowed from an invisible perch.

A car rumble rolled down the gravel road, not unlike the roar of a fighter jet just before you see it.

M did not know whether to wave for help or hide.

The car and its smoke drew closer. M scooched around to the far side of the tree as it passed.

He put his flat hands on his knees and watched the sun rise.

He heard pheasants cackle and mourning doves coo-coo.

M thought about the group home and realized he probably didn't have a job.

He remembered washing dishes after supper with the clients, the radio turned to oldies. They'd be dancing in the kitchen, eating the leftovers off the plates and having water fights with the spray hose.

He remembered sitting outside on summer nights talking to Rosey about politics and the Twins and the best flavors of juice boxes and cigarettes. They'd dream of what it would be like to be tall, or to drive forever on one tank of gas.

He liked working there he guessed. Those were people he felt comfortable with, maybe superior. Maybe that was why he felt comfortable. They sure weren't like other people, but then they *were* just like them. They could drive you crazy with their infant-like questions — and they could give you goose bumps.

# The American Dream

"I do okay. I'm no hero," he said out loud. He wondered if he liked being there because those folks were also outcasts.

"Motley Crue is our friend." M smiled when he recalled what Theresa said one night after listening to oldies on her headphones.

M became hungry.

He stood up by climbing the tree.

He walked off through the grass and the poop and the weeds and the Canadian thistle.

He used a corner post to get over the fence, then jogged down the ditch and out again. He went on along the side of the road, his head down, kicking at rocks and sticks.

M rounded a long curve in the road where it bent back and headed into a long straightaway, in a valley filled with trees and bees and corn and birds.

He stopped at a private drive with a mailbox in the shape of a grain elevator. The lane was sprinkled with woodchips. His stomach rumbled out loud and he dreamed of a stream of cold water pouring from a hose.

M headed down the long drive, swiping at the chips, soccer style, saying "it's good" and raising his hands.

The lane curved around a pond and ran between two rows of aspen trees. A driveway led to a basketball hoop attached to a one-story gray brick home.

M put his palms on the hedge and looked into the window and saw "Walker, Texas Ranger" on the TV screen.

"May I help you?" A melodramatic bull in the pasture to M's left caused him to leave his feet and jump backwards.

"Hey," he said, trying to smile and not succeeding. "Walker," he said, pointing to the window.

"Yes," said the man, "wouldn't miss it in this house. Who might you be, sir?"

The man looked familiar.

A new PitchBlack BJ was parked in the drive.

"I escaped from the prison farm," M pointed across the fields. "I think they call me 'The Big Evil One'. I'm M."

The man grabbed his red suspenders and leaned back to roar.

"Ha! Ha!

"*You* are 'The Big Evil One Asshole Fuck-Shit? You are M?

"I do not mean to insult you, but I'm afraid not."

"Not?" said M to himself.

"Now, who are you and what are you doing in my hedge at seven in the a.m.?"

"Um, I told you."

"Okay, okay. You be M," the man came closer and put his arm around M. "And I'll be Matt Dillon. But tomorrow I get to be M.

"May I offer you some breakfast, coffee? Or do you not need food?"

"I do," said M, letting the man herd him inside.

They walked into the kitchen and sat at the circular counter in the middle of the red and white elegant 1950s "Ma & Pa" farm style kitchen.

A wave of laughter peeled from the other room.

The man went to check.

"Ha! Ha!"

He returned to the kitchen. "Some guy Super-Glued his posterior to the toilet seat. They had it on the news."

The man ran a hand back through his stylishly greased red hair. He had very white skin, and freckles on his face and arms and hands.

He sat a cup of coffee in front of M, and some cereal boxes, bowl, spoon, plastic jug of milk with a blue cap.

# The American Dream

In waltzed a little girl in a pretty white dress with white bows in her red hair. She sat up on the counter next to M as if he were a member of the family.

"Aren't you going to say grace?" she asked M as he began digging in.

M stopped his spoon and held it still in his bowl and bowed his head.

The girl parked her elbows on the table and pressed her hands flat together and leaned her forehead against them.

She closed her eyes.

"Oh, God," she began in a voice that made M smile. "Thank you for the rain and the corn and the farmers, and also for the moisture.

"Oh Jesus ... for the farmers, Oh, God, and also for the corn, and ... the rain. For this we pray, Oh, God, thank you for this day ... and for the farmers.

"Amen, Oh, God."

M renewed working his cereal-scooping dragline.

"You're Mr. M."

"Yep."

"Daddy, here's M!" she sang running into the living room as M slurped.

They walked back into the kitchen holding hands.

"Glory seems to believe you are the man who tried to run her over."

M chewed and looked at him, then the little girl. He recalled the girl in the crosswalk, the Black Blow Job, the crash into the war memorial, the gray pubic hair, the gray heart, the white quarter moon, the white and gray Mohawk.

He stopped chewing.

He swallowed.

"I didn't try to," he said. "I tried not to. The throttle sticks."

"I remember you!" the man howled. His face flooded red. He pointed a finger at M's nose.

"You *are* The Evil One," he hissed.

"Yup."

M shoved his spoon deep into his cereal bowl, which he had refilled.

"Oh my God!" A tall, thin, attractive woman walked into the kitchen and put her hands on her cheeks, as if she were performing a part in a play.

"It's him!

"What is *he* doing here?" She screamed at her husband.

"He's hungry, look at that," said the girl, pointing to the cereal on the counter, in M's lap, on the floor.

"He was outside!" the man said, stuffing cereal boxes into his arms.

"Grab him!" said the woman to the man whose hands were full.

The girl moved in front of M and spread her arms like a crosswalk guard.

"He didn't hit me," she said.

She put her thumb and finger almost together next to her eye to signify "that much."

"Could have, easy," she said.

The man set the boxes back down and put his arm around his wife's shoulders and pulled her close. M stealthily reached for a box he had not yet tried and began to pour while keeping his eyes on the couple.

"Why *are* you here?" asked the man, tired, out of breath.

"I told you," said M, his mouth filled with Homeland Chunks.

"You escaped?"

M nodded, chewing.

# The American Dream

"Why?" asked the man.

"Why?"

"Why would you escape?" said the woman. "You are there for a reason."

"They let me go."

"Ohhh," said the man and woman together.

"I'd like to get registered," said M, wiping his jaw with a Ground God napkin from the pile on the counter.

"Oh, to vote, yeah," said the man. "That's very important. Good for you."

"Mm, mm, TV," said M, pointing to the other room.

"I want to register to be on TV!" said the girl.

"The Home Helper Show," said M.

"We love that show!" The man and woman bent their knees and pointed fingers straight at M.

"That's how we got this kitchen," said the man.

"And the pool," the girl pointed toward the backyard.

"You need to get registered," said the woman.

"I can help you," said the man, "if you'll do something for me."

# Chapter Nineteen

> They don't give a shit how many indigenous, Asian
> or African people get slaughtered. Two thousand,
> two million; they don't give a fuck. They think they
> don't count. There's too many of them; they have
> no feelings, no brain; it's how they think. [...] who
> gave a fuck about Indonesians butchering East
> Timorese? Who cares what happens to Papuans?
> Who cared about how many millions we killed in
> Indo-China? Who cares about millions of people
> dying from AIDS? Who cares about half of the
> population of this planet living in a gutter?
>
> — Andre Vltchek, <u>Point of No Return</u>

On the Westside, on Seventh Avenue, a child lay in the
street, on its side, motionless. His mother sat on the edge of
the road holding the other one.

Next to the mother stood a cardboard cutout of a smiling
man with black hair in a white shirt rolled to his elbows and a
bright red tie, gesturing with thumb tucked inside pointer
finger.

A tape recording played from the cutout:

> We will take on the complicated problem of
> coordinating summertime lawn watering schedules;
> we will stop pre-dawn jaywalking by exercisers. Vote
> for me and help Homeland. My party is dedicated to
> doing whatever it takes to bring justice and peace
> and prosperity!

Sweat dripped down the cardboard candidate.

An F-16 Perpetrator, with a Sun God flag on its side, roared,
still in the distance, and then appeared. In the same instant it
dropped its bombs expertly on the house across the road,
which exploded and caught fire.

# The American Dream

The mother leaned and reached to grab the arm of the child in the street with blood running out its anus, and dragged it closer to her.

Lions yawned in the grass nearby and Raga music drifted down the block.

Down the road came a shining red pickup full of men and women. On the sides were magnetic signs:

**Pastors LOVE Dick**

The ministers chanted and sang and fellowshipped as F-16s, zooming at treetop level, tore up the neighborhood with machine gun fire.

The preachers pointed at the mother struggling to feed one child while pulling her older one out of the path of the oncoming religious leaders. "God loves you, child," they shouted.

"Alleluia!"

"Vote for Dick!"

"Dick and Jane will make it rain!"

The pickup's front tire ran over the child's legs and stopped. The ministers ceased chanting and looked wide-mouthed at the scene behind the woman.

The dead lawns were filled with children, mouths open and stomachs bulging, ribs sticking from tight skin.

The children chewed on bullets, knawing at them from different angles, trying to figure how to eat them. Mothers were sticking M-16 Remington cartridges into the mouths of their children. Stacks of shells for small arms, 20mm F-16 cannon rounds, and large, oblong bombs were placed in neat piles among the dead babies and the infants sucking and choking on the varieties of ammunition.

The Cardboard Cutout Candidate smiled and said: "Daytime lawn watering, jaywalkers, round baseballs, round basketballs."

"How did this happen?" said one of the woman ministers wearing a blue shirt and white collar.

"This yard is a mess!"

"They need to mow."

"Paint this house!"

"And water."

"Pick up the yard."

"Let us pray for these people — right here, right now."

The ministers packed into the bed of the pickup truck bowed their heads and folded their hands at their waists. Some held hands. A couple of them put their open hands up to the sky, laid their heads back as if to drink rainwater and closed their eyes, gently swaying back and forth.

One woman began to hum "Faith of Our Fathers."

"Oh, God, began a male minister from Homeland, "please, thank you, yes sir, no sir. These are the words that made our land strong. What we need is discipline, responsibility, honor and integrity. Today's young people have too much given to them Oh, Lord. We ask that some be taken away, by thy mighty hand. Smite them, dear Jesus, across the mouth."

"Uh, hum, yes," a woman pastor from Franklin stepped in, shoving between two others to reach the edge of the pickup and address the dying people on the lawn.

"Yes, Lord," she shouted, "We *will* kill. We Christians will bomb and rape and steal and lie. We might as well call ourselves tree-trimmers as Christians. We have turned it into a nonsense word. We will destroy the earth with our rapacious avarice, our negligence, our sloth and our apathy.

"We thank you, Jesus, Yahweh, Jehovah, for being there, in our hour of need. When the telephone rings, dear God, and we are outside and we think, please God, don't let them hang up until I get there, and it is my dear child who needs a ride home from swimming, and can I find the keys and where did I

park the car, you were there, with us, Jesus, through all of
that. "Oh, dearest God, for this we pray.

"And we will go to the glittering church in fine clothes and
new shiny BJ, Red, Black, Gold, Silver, AwesomeYellow, and
we will sit there and praise you Lord Jesus Christ, and listen
to the pastor. He dares say nothing about the poor or poverty
or our own riches and home, our bank accounts, our ultimate
concern for our own undisturbed routines — nothing about
building bombs to kill rather than bread to feed and, Oh, God,
we do not remind him. He will never mention Thou Shall Not
Kill or the true spirit of Christianity and this will be repeated
week after week in thousands, millions of churches around
the country and we shall never be bothered with the real you,
Jesus, who would rather see these crystal crappers laid
down brick upon brick and our own phony hearts torn from
our chests, because we are scoundrels, Lord.

"Oh, praise you, Jesus."

"Amen," said the ministers in unison.

The pickup rolled off the legs of the boy.

His mother hauled him onto the coarse grass by one arm
and stared up at the ministers through eyes made large by
the retreating of her skin.

# Chapter Twenty

To live in the process is absolutely not to notice it —
please try to believe me — ... Each step was so
small, so inconsequential, so well explained, or on
occasion, 'regretted'...

> — German university professor,
> describing to journalist Milton Mayer
> what it was like under the Nazis in the
> 1930s

What surprised me at first was that most Germans
... did not seem to mind that their personal freedom
had been taken away, that so much of their splendid
culture was being destroyed and replaced with a
mindless barbarism ... Yet the Nazi terror in those
early years ... affected the lives of relatively few
Germans ... the vast majority did not seem unduly
concerned with what happened to a few
Communists, Socialists, pacifists, defiant priests and
pastors, and to the Jews. ... the people did not
seem to feel that they were being cowed and held
down by an unscrupulous tyranny. On the contrary
... they appeared to support it with genuine
enthusiasm.

> — William Shirer, "Nightmare Years"

The Rapture whistle at the Community Center howled, along
with the sirens of six police cruisers and the horns of a long
line of red and yellow fire department trucks of varied sizes
and shapes.

The Homeland Fourth of July parade was led by elderly
veterans of "The Massacre of Indian Women & Children",

111

# The American Dream

"The Murder of El Salvador" and "The People's Most Honorable And Justified Crucifixion Of The Black Race In Prison".

They limped along, toting Sun God flags and Wind God Flags and Rain God flags, and Ground God flags, dragging along the street the skulls of young Mexican men caught trying to sneak into the country to find a job.

The crowd lounging on the grass yawned and scratched themselves and smelled under each other's underarms for the tell-tale signs of body odor. It rose as the color guard passed their area and sat just as quickly.

The people covered the lawns with colorful plastic chairs and coolers and short pants.

They watched the high school band march by and the Homeland Insurance Co. float.

They ooed and aahhhed as Al Dyka, back country illusionist, entertained the crowd with sleight of hand, making himself appear and disappear. Then it was like he never even existed, as his wife in the tractor pulled along the empty grain wagon.

Car racing sounds hung in the air: zooms and rhooms and screeching tires, from the stock car races being held out on the fairgrounds.

In front of the library, on the sidewalk, an eating contest was ongoing, with television sets and sofas set up.

Along chugged the Dairy Queen and her court float, the Hardware Queen and her attendants, the Rodeo Queen, the Soybean Queen, the Ham Fat Princess and finally the Ethanol Royalty.

Dick & Jane sat with perfect posture high atop the back seat of a cherry red Cadillac.

They wore casual camouflage as they tossed white terror whistles to the children running in packs alongside. Spot sat proudly in the front seat with the driver, ears waving in the breeze.

Next came the Democratic Party float, a bright red pickup adorned with red, white and blue ribbons and bows. In the back, propped up by sparkling, tight bales of straw and Sun God flags, stood The Cardboard Cutout Candidate. Signs made of colored poster board and markers on the sides of the pickup said:

**Daytime Lawn Watering, It's About Time**
**Free Jokes**
**Pro-Corn**
**Pro-Soybeans**

The cutout wore camo, smiled and waved.

During a gap in the lineup, boys dashed back and forth across the street, followed closely by dogs and little sisters.

A roar, a howl, rolled down the street. Folks up by the Freedom Fizz Balloon stand, operated by The Daughters of The Rape of The Phillipines, could see the commotion down toward the park corner. People were standing, pointing, yelling and throwing things at the next float.

A flock of out of breath, shirtless fourth grade boys ran up to the balloon lady. They bent over, grabbed their knees and held their mouths open, unable to talk.

They pointed toward the large golden balloons for one dollar.

As the woman filled they were finally able to blurt in spurts.

"Big Evil.

"One.

"Asshole.

"Shit-fuck."

They pointed.

"M," they said as one.

"M?" The woman put her hands to her cheeks and dropped a balloon on her shoes, then hurried to fill the rest.

The boys collected their rubber bombs and ran down the hill toward the Homeland Elevator entry headed their way.

# The American Dream

The float, a wagon covered with hundreds of crumpled Sun God napkins, was being pulled by a freshly waxed Brand New PitchBlack Shiny Chevrolet Blow Job driven by the big red-haired manager of the elevator, with his wife in the passenger side waving and tossing "Be Afraid" cards to the kids, with black and white photos of Dougs, Homos and People Who Don't Seem To Have Much To Say.

On the wagon was a large kennel cage and inside, gripping the bars, stood M. He wore rose white panties with no shirt or shoes, and held in his hand a black hood, which was really a spray-painted seed corn sack. The floor of the cage was littered with bones, a charred Sun God flag and ripped Bible pages.

The little girl in her white dress sat on her bicycle outside the cage, and every once in a while M reached through the bars as if trying to grab her. The girl would put her hands on her face and squeal "Oh, my!" in her pretty little girl's voice that was everything about freedom and liberty and worshipping wherever you want.

Stuffed into one of her white rose flowered socks she had the ten-dollar bill that her father said was for M and her to get ice cream after the parade.

"Evil!" shouted one older lady in a wide flowered straw hat putting her hand to her mouth. She leaned forward in her pink plastic chair.

"Asshole!"

Her neighbor stood and waved her hand and flabby arm fat at M.

"We are *so* free!" yelled an eighth grade girl eating a baby calf sandwich.

"I *know!* It's so awesome!" said her friend.

The crowd on both sides roared with laughter as a policeman walked into the middle of the road to officiously put up a hand to make the big red-haired man halt his Blow Job.

Then a small pumper truck pulled up next to M's cage and a fireman sprayed M with a stiff, hard stream.

Then the boys with the bombs walked up and fired at M's cage.

Two missed completely.

One broke on a bar and the contents splattered M.

The last one hit M square in the face while he was rubbing his eyes.

The float behind M and the elevator, a large papier-mâché Ten Commandments tablet for the Sun God Summer Bible Camp, backed up ten feet to get out of range.

Shaking his head and laughing, leaning over, holding his gut, the policeman stepped to the side and waved the Homeland Elevator float on.

M stood in the middle of his cage, rubbing his eyes with his fists, trying not to fall as the pickup pulled away. He stumbled, caught himself, then fell back, flat on his back on the wood flooring of the wagon.

He rolled to his side, sweat and Freedom Fizz running down his forehead and nose, into his mouth.

He licked his upper lip and looked into the blue eyes of his little girl, in the arms of his wife standing on the curb.

M's son clutched his mother's leg.

All three stared at M with closed mouths.

M looked back and then waved. His daughter waved back.

They watched each other as the float rolled down the street.

M fought to get to his feet, struggling to climb up the slippery bars.

On his knees he yelled to his wife, "I'm getting us signed up!"

He kept his eyes on his wife until she turned and melted into the crowd.

# Chapter Twenty-one

If it is possible for someone to assassinate a
President in broad daylight in a major American city,
and then have the federal government fake the
autopsy evidence and conceal the nature of the
crime itself, then those who exercised that kind of
power are emboldened to repeat performances of
that kind over and over again. The American people
are not unreasonable to suspect that that has
happened to them many times by now.

— Paul Kuntzler

Mrs. M pushed her kids at the park. Her little home was
somewhere nearby. Then she walked to the post office to
drop something into the mailbox. She brought the kids with
her, both ways, then they swung some more.

I saw it out my basement window.

I wonder if she knows where her husband is, or why, or if she
cares. She looks like she just exists, swings the kids and goes
home. Sometimes her hair is long and sometimes it's in a
ponytail, once pigtails, once a bright red bandana.

My essay is taking too long.

I don't like taking too long to say what shouldn't take very
long, and I don't like saying anything at all if there's nothing to
say.

Friends.

Parents.

Girlfriend.

Religion.

Jesus.

Poverty.

# Mike Palecek

Depression.

I think that's it.

Friends are about the greatest thing, to be part of a group is so cool.

If you have one thought of your own though, keep it to yourself; put it in a dirty gym sock with your semen and throw it way under your bed — if you really, really want to keep that feeling.

Parents. One million books have been written about them. My parents didn't have a clue.

Whatever I learned I found out on my own, by accident. And whatever I learned after that was a series of more accidents, sometimes a pileup, several times just me and the ditch and a pole.

And so on, and so on, and that's kind of how the world works.

Girlfriends. Ahh, ninth grade, that's as good as it gets.

Religion. Oh, Jesus.

Just one tough son of a bitch, with heart.

If you can do what he did you will be going one hundred percent against parents, girlfriend, wife, friends, job — job, that's the other one — well, you won't have one, don't worry about it. You'll be poor and you might get depressed, which is more than being sad. You might end up walking up and down the streets of your hometown on Thursday afternoons in June in your pajamas, only you won't own pajamas.

You'll have gym shorts with the crotch worn away, and you won't be wearing a shirt and shoes, and the old ladies in the windows will call the police and they will come talk to you.

And they will be very nice and condescending, grinning to each other, and you will become angry because who are they to talk to you about anything, about what you are wearing or where you are walking or what thoughts you are having at this very, very moment.

# The American Dream

And being different from all the capitalistic motherfuckers in this goddamn white bread fascist state little fuck town!

And there you have what comes from going to church and going to school and eating whatever they set in front of you and sitting straight.

And that's all those things on the list that make up living in Homeland or anywhere else.

You will either be like exactly everybody else in town and make that your most excellent opportunity goal, or you will hate everybody and you will be the weirdest dude in your own town.

And that is the end of my essay.

Get your ass off my property.

# Chapter Twenty-two

But the rest of you, what are you thinking, reporting on NSA wiretapping or secret prisons in eastern Europe? Those things are secret for a very important reason: they're super-depressing. And if that's your goal, well, misery accomplished. Over the last five years you people were so good — over tax cuts, WMD intelligence, the effect of global warming. We Americans didn't want to know, and you had the courtesy not to try to find out. Those were good times, as far as we knew.

— Stephen Colbert, White House
Correspondents' Dinner, 2006

A thin man, with sparse gray hair poofed out the sides of his gray railroad cap, said darn as his wrench clanked and echoed on the hardwood Community Center floor.

A lone light in the middle of the ceiling cast a faint glow over the large, empty room.

The man kept all manner of wrenches and screwdrivers and hammers and tapes in the pockets of his gray overalls. He strained and leaned into the bolt on the voting machine for Ward One, his white T-shirt soaked through.

A radio sitting on the floor, next to the wall, played Tommy Dorsey and Glenn Miller.

At the end of the cul-de-sac on Disney Avenue, the extended Heavens family sat outside, their lawn chairs in a full circle on the back patio.

Dick and Jane sat in adjoining, full-length red and blue Lounge Lawners. The six children, wearing blaze orange T-shirts and shorts, sat close by in the six-wide, being cooled by a stern grandma with a Sun God cardboard fan.

# The American Dream

Dick and Jane wore matching camouflage golf attire with blaze orange golf shoes. They held hands, handed Freedom Fizz to the others, smiled, laughed and had great fun with their family gathered around.

Three reporters on their knees shouted questions from the front sidewalk.

Dick could hear the commotion, but could not make out the words.

Spot, sitting on the red patio bricks next to Dick and Jane, perked up his ears.

"Brother and sister!" hollered one of the reporters, getting off his knees to scream at the house.

Dick scowled and nodded to a large man nearby with an earphone, wearing black T-shirt, black shorts, black socks and black shoes.

The man nodded to another man, who spoke into a microphone attached to his head, who was speaking to a man on the roof of the Heavens home with a Macintosh laptop.

The man wrote a story for the radio while straddling the peak of the roof. It said the reporter was a gay Muslim fat man who slept with his twin daughters while eating Ho-Ho's in their grandmother's bed on Christmas Eve.

A carload of teenagers in an AwesomeYellow BJ, classmates of the reporter's daughters, came around the circle with the radio blaring, laughing and pointing at the reporter, who sank again to his knees.

"We *will* carry the Westside," said Dick to the group around him.

"I guarantee it," grinned Jane, clinking colored family cups with Dick.

At the Democratic Party headquarters downtown, in the rented former rummage shop storefront, the Cardboard

Cutout Candidate stood in the middle of the room where helpers had set him.

He smiled and extended his hand to shake with anyone in range. Staff members and volunteers paced in a circle around the cutout, holding Styrofoam cups of coffee and nodding to each other seriously.

The circle stopped for a moment as a dying brown baby on the sidewalk howled at a Sun God F-16 flying low overhead. People resumed pacing as the child died and the plane dropped its load on the Westside.

The voting booth for the entire Westside was hauled in by a Homeland maintenance worker with a front-loader. When set down, the aqua blue PortaPoll landed on its side. The worker tossed out an unsharpened pencil and a roll of paper ballots.

M sat on the wagon floor of the cage of the Homeland Elevator Co. float, inside the elevator maintenance shop.

He held his head in his hands, trying to itch his back on the wooden wagon flooring.

The outside door opened.

M saw a brief bright square of light.

"When do I get out of here?" he asked while the big red-haired man was still across the room.

"Hey, I'm headed down to vote," the man called, "get you anything?"

"You said you would get me registered."

"Yes, yes. There's time for that. Did you see the fireworks last night? No, I guess you didn't. Pretty awesome."

"I heard it," said M. "Can you get me a hamburger, fries?"

The man shot both pointer fingers at M.

M stood to say, "And a strawberry malt?"

# The American Dream

"Listen, M, as soon as we do a couple more parades, some county fairs, then we'll get you all signed up. How 'bout that?"

The man strolled toward the door with his head down, hands in his pockets.

"Yeah. Sure. Can you ask for extra ketchup … please?"

M sat down in the middle of the wagon. He leaned back on his hands and stretched his legs out.

The door opened and slammed shut.

The polling places at the Eastside churches and the Community Center did a steady business throughout the morning.

Some citizens had set up the Westside polling station and sharpened the pencil.

Voters had begun to take their turn, tearing off a square and dropping their votes into the receptacle.


M waited until after noon in the sauna of the metal elevator machine shed.

He realized the big red-haired man had forgotten his malt.

He tried fitting his head between the bars. He tried eating the straw.

He heard scattered fireworks still going off around town.

"We are so free," M said out loud to himself.

"That our flag was still there," he sang.

M lay on his back listening to the pigeons.

The door squeaked open and whammed shut.

M thought, "it's about time."

"Hey," the little girl squeaked.

M sat up.

"Hey."

"Just a minute," she said.

She put a foot on one of the big tires and worked hard and grunted and gripped the top of the wagon.

"Careful," said M.

The girl fought to pull herself up by the edge. She got her face above the floor, just hanging on by her fingertips.

She gripped the ten-dollar bill in her teeth. She nodded with her chin to suggest that M take the money.

Then she let herself down and backed up to be able to see M. She pointed to a pile of clothes she had placed by the wagon. Without warning she wound up and fired a ring of keys at M, striking him square in the stomach.

"It's one of them," she said. "There wasn't going to *be* any ice cream. I talked to my cousin Rosey. You need to get out of here."

"This is so lame." She held out her arms to encompass everything.

The girl pivoted on the toe of her black patent leather shoe and headed for the door.

# Chapter Twenty-three

"Live one day at a time. Say 'if this isn't nice, I don't know what is.' "

"You meet saints everywhere. They can be anywhere. They are people behaving decently in an indecent society."

"Well ... I just want to say that George W. Bush is the syphilis president.

"The only difference between Bush and Hitler, is that Hitler was elected.

"You all know, of course, that the election was stolen. Right here."

> — Kurt Vonnegut, speaking at Ohio State University

M appeared at the door of the elevator maintenance building, peering through a crack out at the town: cars moving slowly down Main Street, kids on bikes, a Mexican couple walking holding pinky fingers.

Grind Zero, that's where he was, where it all started, when the elevator was attacked by midget aliens flying remote control airplanes. They had made it explode and fall down, so Dick had no choice but to bomb the Westside, and ban public speaking and private conversations.

"I love this land," said M to himself, out loud.

He wore his old clothes, the ones given to him that night the guard let him go.

M needed to get registered for the Homeland segment of The Home Helper Show, so he could get his kitchen remodeled, an addition put on, the bathroom made larger, and a pool with clear water and bubbles.

He needed to get to his house and talk to his wife.

He pushed open the door, all the way.

"One small step for man, a larger step for ..." he mumbled.

M walked down Main Street, his head held high, back straight, anticipating direct eye contact.

He noticed the new "Stop, Drop & Roll" billboard atop the bakery.

He did not wish to be re-captured by the elevator manager. He had heard him talking about the circus. But he felt he could outrun the big red-haired man in an open field, and at the end of the day what he really needed was to get on with his life, turn the next page.

He stopped to look in the window of Bradley's Clothing Store to admire the new skins, light brown reversible jackets. The sign next to the display said: "Look for the illegal label. 100% Mexican, made in Arizona."

M shook his head.

He'd never be able to afford one of those. He didn't even have a job.

M headed down the street, past the bakery, the Community Center, the library, the bookstore.

He saw his own face on some of the **Be Afraid** signs along the sidewalk and resolved to turn his life around, to make his family proud of him. Maybe he could be a coach, a youth minister, or scout leader.

He marched straight toward his own little house, turning right on Liberty Avenue, on two blocks, left at Freedom.

A block from his home M could smell the familiar apple pies sitting in the kitchen windows of the houses. Each home was shiny white with a Sun God flag snapping from the front porch. Plastic children's toys in primary colors littered the front lawns of most of the residences.

# The American Dream

Each lawn spread full and emerald. Fathers in white T-shirts and dress slacks sipped Freedom Fizz brought outside to them by smiling wives in black high heels sporting crisp red and white fluffy dresses.

"I love this town," said M to himself.

He smiled and waved to his neighbors watching him suspiciously.

M saw his next-door buddy and walked over to visit with him as he knelt in his lawn reading his Bible and shining his grass with a chamois.

"Hey!" M raised his hand.

Without speaking, staring M in the eyes, the man pointed a garden hose at M. He stuck his thumb in the stream and shot it into M's eyes.

M clamped his eyes, put up his hands, turned around and walked away.

M headed down the sidewalk toward his house.

The neighbor's two little children ran up behind him.

M turned and smiled. He bent down to say hello to the tiny boy and girl.

They drew back and each fired an egg at M, hitting him in the face and shoulder. They turned and ran away, across the grass to their house, churning their little legs and pumping their chubby arms and fists as if the devil was right behind.

M stood and watched them as he wiped his face and clothes.

He turned again toward his house. He fought against tears when he saw his wife's plucky little red and yellow and white chrysanthemums in the front plot under the window.

The white house needed painting and so did the garage. Shingle bits littered the weedy flowerbeds. The driveway was cracked and the gutters still held last fall's leaves.

M walked to the side door back by the garage and tried it. He came around to the front door, locked as well. He leaned around over the front railing to look in the window, and saw the house was dark except for the bathroom light.

A bear and a Baby Doll with just her top on were on the floor next to some toy cups and dishes. Also scattered around were books, green and orange Sippy cups, a spoon half-full of peanut butter, Care Bears tapes and "Finding Nemo."

M straightened up, put his hands on his hips and put his head down to think.

Maybe she was out voting.

He could wait and then call to get registered or however you do it.

M turned around and sat down on the front cement porch steps. He reached for a concrete chip and tossed it at the open garbage can his wife had set out for pickup.

"It's good," he said, and made crowd noise by putting his hand over his mouth and breathing hard.

M picked egg shell off his shirt and looked up.

On his front sidewalk stood a line of his neighbors.

They stared hard with hands on hips.

One of the men held a cell phone to his ear.

"He's here, right now," the man said.

"They're on their way," he said to the others as he slapped the phone closed.

"We should shoot him," said one of the women.

"Shoot him?" said another woman while reaching up to touch one earring.

"Who's got a gun?" asked a man with a broad white mustache and narrow head.

"We've got lots," said a younger man with short hair and long, dark sideburns. He put up a hand to say everyone stay put as he hopped into a sprint toward his house.

M got up and walked a few steps toward his neighbors.

# The American Dream

"You're going to shoot me?" he asked, still plucking egg shells from his shirt.

A short, stocky man from two doors north nodded.

"Thinkin' about it," an athletic middle-aged woman in pigtails stepped to the front.

"Because ...," M began.

"Becauuse ... you are dangerous!" hollered a large woman in bare feet, her face turning red. "You are evil," she hummed, the words seeming to come out of her large eyes pinned on M.

"You are The Evil Big One!"

"Asshole!"

"Shit-fuck."

M heard jingling, clinking, and scraping and looked to see his neighbor hustling over, trying to carry a shotgun, two rifles, along with a hunting knife in his teeth.

M walked up another couple of steps and watched the man pass out the weapons.

"Some are going to have to share," he said, hurrying to getting everything arranged, dropping shells and bullets on the sidewalk, losing them in the grass and scrambling to match the right ammunition with the right weapon.

"Somebody go first," said the woman with the skinning knife.

"We need an ice breaker," someone said.

"Someone shoot him. I don't think I should stab him first, that should come later."

"Of course," another nodded in agreement. "I agree," said another.

One of the men raised a rifle to his shoulder and aimed at M's face.

M stared back like a deer unsure of what he was seeing.

A siren cried out and a black and white police car squealed around the corner. Behind the police, with its flashers on, gunned a Brand New Shiny PitchBlack Chevrolet Blow Job.

Down the street from the other way came M's wife, sparks flying as the station wagon frame scraped the bump in the intersection.

She slowed up way before reaching the group.

M turned and ran around behind his house through the back yard, into the alley, and was into another neighborhood being chased by an intelligent young black labrador before the police and the big red-haired guy and his wife climbed out of their vehicles.

M's wife pulled to the curb, across the street. She stood for a moment in the road with her door open. She held her arm stiffly extended back into the car to keep the kids inside. She gathered her long hair in her hand and pulled it over her shoulder, keeping her eyes on the activity, trying to figure it all out, then pulled on her hair again, for smooth and straight.

The policeman and the elevator manager walked up to the crowd, now a circle, and asked what was going on.

They told the men they had spotted M. The policeman hurried back to his car to radio for help. The big red-haired man visited with the neighbors, trying to find out where M had disappeared to. No one had seen him run off. The man looked up into the trees, down the sidewalk, back at the house.

The big man stood outside the circle, hands on his hips, looking around, trying to figure it all out.

He spotted M's wife still standing by her car. She looked at him. Their eyes met. She gripped her hair in one hand and with the other she formed a pistol that pointed toward the back alley.

# Chapter Twenty-four

How many people do you have to kill before you
qualify to be described as a mass murderer and a
war criminal? One hundred thousand? More than
enough, I would have thought. Therefore it is just
that Bush and Blair be arraigned before the
International Criminal Court of Justice. ...

The United States supported and in many cases
engendered every right wing military dictatorship in
the world after the end of the Second World War. I
refer to Indonesia, Greece, Uruguay, Brazil,
Paraguay, Haiti, Turkey, the Phillipines, Guatamala,
El Salvador, and of course, Chile. The crimes of the
United States have been systematic, constant,
vicious, remorseless, but very few people have
actually talked about them.

You have to hand it to America. It has exercised a
quite clinical manipulation of power worldwide
while masquerading as a force of universal good.
It's a brilliant, even witty, highly successful act of
hypnosis.

— Harold Pinter, Nobel Prize for
Literature Lecture, Dec. 7, 2005


A man with a dark brown weathered face crouched on his
haunches on the sidewalk outside the used clothing store, like
a cat who had seen some things.

He sat with friends, but not too close. He watched the cars
go by as if looking for his mother.

The man wore boots and jeans and a clean old western shirt.

He wore no cap, but the shades of his forehead suggested he knew where to find one. His hair was dark as the ocean bottom and recently combed to the side.

One of the other men said something and the man grinned wide, showing good, white teeth and gullies in his forehead and at the corners of his eyes. A passerby, while fearing to stare too long, felt the depth of the man's suffering.

He rested one hand on a knee with ease that implied he could sit that way for a long time. In his strong, calloused hand, without looking at it, he gently played with something, maybe a baby's rattle or a detonator pin.

The little girl in the white dress walked on the other side of the street, away from the men. She marched with her eyes straight and her fists balled, intent on reaching Homeland Pharmacy.

She took a big step up and pushed open the glass door that chimed. She smiled at the two women behind the front counter and plowed on.

The pharmacist, in his nest in back, smiled at the little girl, who did not see him or the new "Greatest Generation" display with its gas pills, support hose and socks, funeral home business cards, toupee glue, pubic hair 'sculpting' trimmer, eye patches, binoculars, walkers, canes, magnifying glasses, strawberry laxatives, memory pills, forgetting capsules, breath mints, lime and orange room freshener, hand and arm makeup, bedside denture glasses, Depends, toilet bowl cleaner, and Hiroshima postcards.

One of the front desk women rushed to the window to watch a pair of F-16 Baby Rapers whoosh over, the Sun God flag clearly visible on their fuselages. "Your son waved at me!" she said.

They grabbed the counter to steady themselves as the bombs exploded.

"That Rusty," said the man in back in light blue uniform top, turning down Paul Harvey for just an instant. "He's always

# The American Dream

busy, rushing here and there. I'll bet you don't know he's got a softball game tonight and church council."

"Oh, my," said one of the women.

"I don't think Annie's going to get any lawn work out of him tonight," said the man.

"Keeps him out of trouble!" the other woman hollered and smiled.

The pharmacist smiled and nodded and turned the radio up.

One woman returned to straightening the patterns while the other went to help the little girl reach the peppermints.


A postal carrier connected something magnetic under a car on the street and another of the same to the underside of a black mailbox.

M walked past in a hurry and asked with his eyes what she was doing.

"Counters," said the woman. "Tells how fast I get the mail delivered. Always something, damn UPS, you know?"

"Yep, I guess," said M, hurrying, trying not to run, taking every alley and empty street.

He hit the deck when his grandparents cruised proudly by in their gray antique Studebaker. It looked like a mini-submarine. M leaned way into a hedge and hugged the alley floor gravel until they gradually passed.

M rolled to his back. Not a cloud.

He put up his arm to shield his eyes. He pulled his wet shirt free of his chest for a moment.

He looked up and saw John the Baptist moving past in a hurry, wearing sun glasses, Indians ball cap, long shorts, white socks to his knees, and sandals.

Without stopping, John glanced at M, lying in the alley, at his age, in his hometown, in the middle of the afternoon.

"Jesus H. Christ," said John and shook his head, leaning slightly forward, intent.

M rolled over and pushed himself to stand.

He turned at the sidewalk the opposite way that John was headed.

He came to a driveway, wide, smooth and new, where three children had planted a lemonade stand.

They had white and pink and flowered paper cups and an umbrella for shade.

The two boys and one girl looked up at M, eyes wide, not daring to breathe, hoping for a sale.

M remembered two quarters before he was arrested. His hands remembered, too, and dived into both pockets. He smiled. Each hand pulled out a quarter. M dropped them with a chink into the flowered cup marked "Cash" in pencil.

"You're the first," one boy announced. "My mom said it would draw more people in if we had money already in the change cup."

"Credibility," said the girl. "But how do they see into the cup from their car?" She put up her hands around her shoulders and tilted her head. "I dunno."

"You get two glasses," said the other boy, "is that enough?"

"Yep," said M. "One of each." He pointed at the white and the pink.

"Nice day," said the girl while the boys poured. "No clouds, is there?"

"Never is, it seems," said M.

The girl arched her eyebrows and shrugged her shoulders and raised her hands upside down.

M heard a car idling behind him and looked at the children. They stared with wide eyes past M into the street. M peeked over his shoulder.

# The American Dream

A young policeman climbed hatless out of his black and white patrol car. He shut the door while smiling at the children and headed around the front of his vehicle.

M turned back toward the table and took his drinks in his hands, wondering what to do.

"You're all under arrest!" the policeman shouted.

"Daddy!" the little girl screamed. She pushed back her chair and ran around the table into the man's arms.

He tossed her up and caught her, then walked with her fist inside one hand, digging into his pocket with the other.

"How much?" he said.

M sipped white lemonade while walking, hurrying along, hearing the policeman chat with the kids.

As he passed the police car he heard through the open window, "The M Group has just been stopped in the act of destroying lawns in the neighborhood of Freedom and Liberty. The Dick Heavens administration is attributing this to the vigilance of a local 'We're Watching You' neighborhood group."

The radio squawked and the dispatcher continued to read the release after M could no longer hear.

"M Group has also been thwarted in past days from switching the pills at Time's Up nursing home as well as over-watering the fourth and ninth tees at Family Values Golf Club."

"That man bought two." The girl worked to hold up two fingers just right.

The policeman looked at M, now walking away in the shade of a large elm tree.

"Well then, I'll have two, too," he said, setting his coins on the table while keeping his eyes on M.

M alternated sips — white, pink, white — trying to find out if they tasted different. When they were gone he crunched the cups and put them in his front pockets.

## Mike Palecek

M stopped and tried to plan his route, how he could get to the group home without being caught.

He needed to see if he could get his job back, and also watch their TV to learn how to get registered, and then he could go back and find his wife and get a new pool and the driveway patched.

He could go through some more alleys, then at the stop light by Quicke Shop he would cross the highway and then through the park — then the church parking lot and he was almost there.


M chose a shaded street with large elm trees and big front lawns that put any eyes in front windows a ways away.

He walked down the sidewalk as if continually scratching his head or nose or forehead. He watched his feet.

If a car passed he stopped to examine never-before-discovered species of bugs or lawn or igneous rock. To make it more authentic he mumbled to himself, "There must have been a volcano here at one time," as the pickup passed.

He looked up from his squat, feeling someone watching him.

He saw, framed in the front door screen, a naked woman.

She had been a cheerleader for the football and basketball squads during M's senior year.

"Oh, my, Bobbi."

"Michael," she said.

"M," she hummed.

She pushed the screen open with a toe and M saw the mysteries of seventh period science revealed.

Her long black hair was tossed over one shoulder. She ran one hand down the hair and cupped one breast with the other, then petted herself below, with the grain.

M thought she might be making moaning sounds.

# The American Dream

He looked behind him.

He looked back at her.

She was now bent over with her backside facing him, moving it around and back and forth. She had one finger sticking into herself and running it slowly in and out.

She then turned around and stood facing M.

"Want to come, inside, M?"

She licked her finger.

"I can still do splits. I'll make you a strawberry malt. You're hot."

M got up and walked to the house.

He stood at the base of the wooden steps with one hand on the metal railing.

Up close her skin was something smooth and luscious, not tanned, thick. It lay on her frame loosely, not fat, like the skin of a lioness. Her neck was layered from luxury, her lips red, and her lower part seemed to be breathing, heaving, longing for M.

She stared down at M sadly, already sensing his answer.

"I have to be going," he said. "I need to get registered. You look great. Everything is perfect, really. I just need to get registered, really, I do."

"You political types are so devoted," she said. "I didn't vote. You are a dangerous man, M. Come here."

He patted the railing and turned around and told each leg in turn to get moving.

"No," he mumbled to himself, "it's a TV show."

He reached the walk, turned right and heard the screen slam and the inside door rub on the carpet as it closed.


M walked into the road and stopped in the middle.

He heard the bottom of a vehicle scraping against an intersection rise in the road. He swiveled like a TV cop and saw the white knuckles of his wife's hands at eleven and one.

Next he saw the red glow of her eyes like an animal at night, and then the glint as the front of the car reflected the sun and his own image.

Like a runner diving for home M leaped for the nearest lawn, snatching his legs from the street just as his wife knifed past.

He rolled to his side in time to see his two children and their new puppy looking at him out the back window, without emotion, as if M had drained each drop of joy from their veins by his antics.

The tires of the station wagon screeched as Mrs. M slammed on the brakes to complete a U-turn at the next intersection for another sortie.

M got up and took one step the other way.

He saw the Black BJ blocking the sidewalk with emergency flashers blinking.

He stopped in his tracks and stared with open hands outstretched in two directions. The big man climbed slowly out of his vehicle. M heard his wife's tires screaming again, trying to get up enough steam to jump the curb and flatten him.

M searched for an outlet.

He threw his hands into the air and ran around a house, into its back yard, across another, over a street, into an alley, and kept going. He did not stop until he had crossed the highway, shirt tail flying, arms waving, hair streaming, shoes untied.

He found another alley and took it, as if following a railroad track through occupied territory, or a river past a blazing forest fire.

He dived headfirst into a large, luscious patch of peony bushes, white, pink and red.

# The American Dream

M lay inside the stalks and stems, smelling the flowers, hearing his heart pump, the constant sparse traffic on the highway, and the lights clicking from red to green to yellow.

He heard the chatter of a group of boys sitting on their bicycles outside the Quicke Shop, and the pinging of the pumps. He smelled gas, then cigarette smoke when the attendant snuck out back for a quick break.

M rolled over and found a way to rest kind of comfortably inside the peonies. He folded his hands on his stomach and looked up at the blue sky and closed his eyes at the brightness.

One sparse, disorganized cloud shuffled up. For one instant it partially shielded the sun, and M opened an eye to see scores of blackbirds headed West to roost.

M fell asleep for a moment or an hour.

He woke up to the grinding of car tires over gravel.

He heard the cackle of a police radio.

His back hurt.

He wondered why he was sleeping in peony bushes.

He raised a hand stealthily to part the stalks. He saw, parked in the alley right beside him, a black and white Homeland Police car. M held his breath as long as he could, then let it out in such a torrent he thought sure it would bring another helicopter.

The car door opened, but did not close.

The radio dispatcher talked about an accident "without injuries" at Fourth and Cranberry Jam.

M heard crunching and the sound of metal, clanking, zipping.

"Aaah, shit, wowah," M heard.

He felt warm liquid splashing on his face, smelling like Freedom Fizz. It tasted like it, too. He shut his mouth and eyes and tried to close his nose.

M opened his eyes and gulped air when it stopped.

Then a rush of dribbles hit him square in the mouth. He tried not to taste.

M heard zipping and clanking and crunching and the door slamming. The car slowly rolled away.

M pulled up his shirt to wipe his face.

He heard a television through an open kitchen window and plopped to his side. He peeked out into the alley, knelt to pop his head up through the flowers.

He stood and moved off along the grassy edge of the alley, next to the garages and tool sheds.

# Chapter Twenty-five

Here comes the helicopter — second time today
Everybody scatters and hopes it goes away
How many kids they've murdered only God can say
If I had a rocket launcher ... I'd make somebody pay

I don't believe in guarded borders and I don't believe
in hate
I don't believe in generals or their stinking torture
states
And when I talk with the survivors of things too
sickening to relate
If I had a rocket launcher ... I would retaliate

On the Rio Lacantun, one hundred thousand wait
To fall down from starvation — or some less
humane fate
Cry for Guatemala, with a corpse in every gate
If I had a rocket launcher ... I would not hesitate

I want to raise every voice — at least I've got to try
Every time I think about it water rises to my eyes.
Situation desperate, echoes of the victims cry
If I had a rocket launcher ... Some son of a bitch
would die

> — Bruce Cockburn,
> "If I Had A Rocket Launcher"

M stood in the driveway, looking at the Sun God group home, hands on hips, trying to imagine the taste of strawberry ice cream. It was time for evening snack. Most of the lights were on, in the office and rooms.

M heard music coming from an open window. He walked up a few steps. He crouched and inched ahead, behind a bush, around the bush, to Rosey's screen window.

He could hear her inside singing along. He scratched the screen with his fingernails.

She kept singing. He scratched louder.

The music stopped. He scratched.

"Yes?"

He put his hand to his mouth to expunge a giggle and scratched again.

"Booga-booga-booga. Go away, come back another day."

He scratched again.

She repeated her incantation, pleading. He burst out laughing.

"Hey! Rosey, it's me. C'mere, c'mere."

"Michael?"

"Yes."

"Where are you?"

"Over *here!*"

Rosey appeared in the screen. "I thought you were a ghost."

"Ghost?"

"The state was here," she said. "Inspection. We got gigged for having ghosts. Stupid. Al and Mickey were playing paint gun wars in the house and ran when the inspector came in. Something about doors moving and sounds. I think the inspector was nuts. But then I heard you. What are you doing? I thought you were in Saudi Arabia, they said. They say you're the head of the terrorists, The Big Evil One. I never did believe that, they're nuts."

"I need to get registered," he whispered.

"Voting's over," she said, pushing her head into the screen. "I didn't vote for The Cardboard Cutout or Dick Heavens. I wish you were on the ballot."

# The American Dream

"Me? I need to get signed up for The Home Helper Show. How do you do that? I think I can get on the show if I can just get signed up."

"I signed up a hundred times," said Rosey. "So did everybody else. You get coupons from the paper or at Quicke Shop. I've got a whole drawer. I'll send one in for you. You want me to?"

"Yeah. That'd be great," said M. "A hundred? Everybody?"

"Yep. Where you gonna sleep? You still work here? I don't know."

Rosey pulled back from the screen. M could see the pattern in her forehead.

"I wouldn't come inside," she said. "They think you're ... how's that go?"

"Fuck-shit something," he said.

"Shit-fuck! That's it.

"You could sleep in the corn on the other side."

"Yeah."

"Or the beans," she said.

"If you hide in corn you can stand up, but in soybeans you must lie down. You probably already know that."

"Thanks."

"Well, g'night."

"Yep."

# Chapter Twenty-six

Bush, who appeared almost playful, fastened the heavy medal around Muhammad Ali's neck and whispered something in the heavyweight champion's ear. Then, as if to say 'bring it on,' the president put up his dukes in a mock challenge. Ali, 63, who has Parkinson's disease and moves slowly, looked the president in the eye — and, finger to head, did the 'crazy' twirl for a couple of seconds.

The room of about 200, including Cabinet secretaries, tittered with laughter. Ali, who was then escorted back to his chair, made the twirl again while sitting down. And the president looked visibly taken aback, laughing nervously.

> — Account in the *Washington Post* of Medal of Freedom award ceremony at the White House, Nov. 10, 2005; an accompanying photo shows President George W. Bush pinning the medal on Andy the sheriff from the popular 1960 TV sitcom "Mayberry RFD".

M lay down face-first in the perfect soft half circle of a corn row bed.

He rested his head on his arms.

He closed his eyes and did not notice Bigfoot tiptoeing nearby, or the double quad dual exhaust of a spaceship from Mars on its way to Cruise Night on Pluto. He did not hear the ghosts of Benjamin Franklin and Thomas Jefferson churning in their graves. He slept as Dick and Jane Heavens drank strawberry daiquiris on their deck, and while shadows from the Westside ventured across the railroad tracks.

# The American Dream

The rooster sun crowed.

Small brown birds bounced along the corn rows, chirping, speaking a different language from the black birds balancing on the premature corn ears. Large predators were already patrolling the sky, silent and alone, eyes cast downward.

M woke with his face in the mud. He rolled to his back and then sat up.

He heard church bells ringing, radios playing in kitchen windows and old ladies, gobs of toilet paper in their fists, singing through open bathroom windows.

"Yaay! Praise be the Sun God! Dick Heavens, for more years!"

M pulled himself up by a stalk, stood and looked across a sea of corn just as tall as he.

Out in the country, he could see a farmer and a tractor poofing smoke. He wondered how he might get registered a few more times.

"Sound off, one-two. Sound off, three-four," M sang to himself.

He sat down again in the row.

With his finger he drew in the dirt:

**All gave some, some gave all.**

He expounded to the attentive ears of corn:

> It's not true that politicians don't care about the truth, that they are only interested in power and in the maintenance of that power.

He retraced his dirt epigram.

> That's what some say, but it's not so.

> It's not easy to be a leader, to have everyone bitching, watching every move you make.

> We're just lucky anybody wants to do it. We should be happy with whatever they do.

It's like those parents on the sidelines who complain about the coaches. They yell at them, follow them home, call them up late at night.

I am not going to be one of those.

M stood again in the corn, looking around, wondering if he could make it to the Quicke Shop and get registered without being captured for the circus.

# Chapter Twenty-seven

I think it's in young people's hands to learn about things, to question what makes no sense, to remember that the world is much bigger, much more beautiful than the frontiers of the U.S., and that the U.S. isn't "America". America is two continents, from Canada to the southern cone of Argentina and Chile, [...] the American continents are part of a big and beautiful world that we will wind up destroying if we don't look to change the way we relate to one another and to the world itself.

I'd say read, inquire, doubt, investigate, dream — but don't sit still, and don't believe that just because the U.S. is the most powerful country on the globe right now, that everything it did to become so was right, and that everything it does to remain as such is also right. Human values, brotherly love and solidarity are more important than greed. There's a lot to do if this world is to continue functioning. Please do something to make it a better place.

> — Lori Berenson, Penal de Huacariz,
> Cajamarca, Peru, 23 April 2005

A cockatoo clung to an overturned bookshelf in the ransacked bookstore. A monkey sat in a broken window, wondering whether to come in or go out.

Outside on the dirt road kids played soccer with a ball of knotted rags.

An old woman sat under a baobab tree stroking the thin hair of a gaunt child. The girl's cheek bones stuck from her skin like a nose into a window screen.

## Mike Palecek

The child did not speak but looked out at the world with big wide eyes. She lay on the ground, her head in the old woman's lap, the bones of her legs in a skewed figure four. Ants crawled on her calloused heels.

The girl's bony chest raised and lowered slowly. She looked all around at the cats, the lion cubs, the jets in the sky, the leftover election signs and the cloudless blue sky, trying to take it all in.

A one hundred boxcar train roared past on the tracks, blowing its whistle. The cockatoo squawked and the monkey chattered and scurried from the sill, up an elm tree.

A cat howled somewhere in the neighborhood.

A line of sweat grew down the old woman's wrinkled forehead onto the closed lips of the child.

The elevator dryers hummed a happy tune.


The bells of an ice cream truck jingled over near Freedom and Liberty as the old woman raised her face to the sun and shrieked.

Tears climbed down her cheeks.

She gently closed the young girl's eyes.

She clenched her hands into fists and gritted her teeth.

Boom!

On the Eastside, in the neighborhood of Honor Avenue and Fourteenth Street, a cream mini-van sat lifeless, smoldering in the middle of the street.

Inside, the seats and roof and mom and dad and brother and sister and fastened seatbelts blazed bright, like Roman candles.

Rich black smoke poured from the hulk.

Metal and parts and rubber and ball glove and Baby Doll and Happy Meal littered the cement and yards around.

# The American Dream

Sirens and lights and screams and people with hands on their cheeks raced toward the red glare of the bonfire.

The old woman knelt to slide her arms under the girl never to hold her own child.

She pulled the girl to her breast and stood strong. She walked barefoot over the sparse lawn and thorns, across the dirt road and out into a dry, hard field.


A young boy of ten, looking like a six-year-old, lay on a bed in his family's front room. All around him relatives knelt and sat as his father led the rosary.

The boy joined the refrain as long as he could, then listened, then slept.

When his father finished he walked over to his only son to feel his chest. The man dropped his head to his breast. The mailbox of a brick home exploded, flattening the house and ripping to bloody strips and chunks a Siamese, a Dalmatian and a retired couple, all seated in the air-conditioned living room, watching TV and nibbling burnt almond ice cream.

At about the same time, maybe a few minutes later, a baby passed away from malnutrition in a grass hut in the country, and the Homeland Bank & Trust was instantly turned into an untidy mass of metal and glass and paper, into brick bits and dust and teeth chips, and parts of skull and femur and crispy burned white skin.


All through the night, as children died on the Westside, explosions immediately followed on the Eastside, including five more homes and seven BJs.

An elderly couple with stately gray hair and a winter home in Phoenix, out for a night stroll, exploded from timed devices in the elastic of their Depends. Their heads rolled down the street before bumping into the arms.

The limbs provided a perch for the neighborhood crows until daybreak.

# Chapter Twenty-eight

"The FBI has 'no hard evidence' connecting Usama
Bin Laden to 9/11 ... Think about it."

— Ed Haas, *The Muckraker Report*

"They hate our big American breasts!"

Newly re-elected Homeland Mayor Dick Heavens stood on the
two front steps of the post office with his fist in the air.

He wore a blaze orange vest over his camouflage business
suit. His orange hunting cap had the flaps down, battle mode.

> We are protecting you from these terrorists by
> listening to your conversations at the cafe. If you
> have nothing to hide, what does it matter?

> They want to take your freedoms away. We want to
> be able to allow you to have even more freedom!

> The Sun God bless Homeland!

> 4-11!

> We are searching for M, the mastermind of the
> attacks, who also was the planner for four-one-one
> and the sit-down rebellion!"

The woman on the street in front of Dick got tired of waiting
for him to get out of the way, and moved along down the
sidewalk.

A blast from downtown, in front of the bakery, blew to bits an
old couple barely moving in a Shiny New Ford. It also took out
the front windows of the Corn Dog Restaurant and brought
down the movie theater marquee.

As Dick raised a finger to make another point a bomb under
the right field bleachers at the ball field sprayed pop and
popcorn and bloody, oozing body parts onto the home team
dugout roof and over the bullpen and first base coaching box.

# Chapter Twenty-nine

| Ron Kovic | We went to Vietnam to stop communism! ... We shell woman and children! |
|---|---|
| Mrs. Kovic | You didn't shoot women and children! What are you saying? |
| Ron Kovic | That was the war, communism, the insidious evil! They told us to go. |
| Mrs. Kovic | Yes, yes that's what they told us. |
| Ron Kovic | Thou shall not kill, Mom. Thou shall not kill women and children! Thou shall not kill! Remember? Isn't that what you taught us? Isn't that what they taught us? |
| Mrs. Kovic | Stop it! Stop it! |

– "Born on the Fourth of July," 1989

The morning of The Homeland Home Helper Show drawing ceremony dawned with one gray, fluffy cloud in the sky.

"Come, Spot, come."

Dick patted his thigh to coax his dog into the garage.

Spot looked Dick in the eye and squatted in the front lawn.

"No, Spot! No!" said Dick.

He waited for Spot to finish and held the side garage door open for the dog to trot inside. He then walked out to his lawn with a Clean Fresh Baggie.

John from the underground drank coffee while watching the morning traffic out his basement window.

# Mike Palecek

Rosey the Riveter sat at the breakfast table with the others, a cell phone to her ear, putting the network into motion.

M sat in the quiet stillness of a forgotten boxcar on an offline spur on the Westside.

He sat against the wall in a corner, enjoying the morning sun through the half open sliding door, reading an old paper. He was boiling his water for coffee in a tin can, and trying not to even look at the pack of rolls he had retrieved from the bakery Dumpster the night before.

His plan was to wait for the coffee.

M tried on the charcoal gray felt hat, with gray band and only a small hole at the top, that he had found on a recent night walk around the Eastside. He arranged the top crease just right with his thumb and first two fingers.

He slipped out one roll from the pack, shoved it all into his mouth and sat back with his head against the boxcar wall, then licked his fingers in turn.

He sang out loud, "A little dab'll do ya."


From all directions, all the sidewalks and alleys and streets, streams of people moved toward the Homeland Elementary School gymnasium.

Kids rode bikes and old people shuffled along on walkers tricked out with tennis balls.

Farmers drove into town in pickups and three-wheelers. Young couples hustled along pushing double- and triple-wide strollers.

M climbed down from the boxcar after straightening his paper bag bed, washing out his cup and tin and burning his garbage.

Dick and Jane arrived at the elementary school outside kitchen door. Inside they were introduced to the lovely young Home Helper Show cast.

# The American Dream

"At the end of the day," said one of the cast members wiping his head, "it's not the heat, so much."

"Bottom line — it's the humidity!" Dick and Jane crouched and fired four pointer fingers at the cast members.

They chatted in the kitchen, amid bun boxes and fifty gallon trays of mac & cheese and weenie casserole, waiting for the time to make their entrance.

M joined the sidewalk brigade wearing his new hat.

At the front walk entrance, where all the streams came together, he saw his wife and children headed inside. He fell in behind, and followed them into the gymnasium filled with about a million gray metal folding chairs.

They found seats in the middle.

M followed them as if they were together and slipped into the row right behind.

Rosey marched down the sidewalk with Sanndra, Theresa, Joseph, Krystal and Mickey. Other members of their troupe joined them at each intersection.

At 10 a.m., the elementary school principal Carol "Soup" Campbell checked her wristwatch against the clock on the kitchen wall above the three-compartment sink.

"Shall we?" She smiled at Dick and Jane and the lovely young cast checking their makeup in the stainless steel refrigerator, and guided them out of the kitchen, across the lunch room to the door in the hall that led to the stage.

Soup put up one finger that meant "just one minute, please."

She went through the door to check the crowd and the seating arrangements and the podium and stuff.

She nodded to the new band director who raised his chin in return then tapped on a music stand. "One, two, three." He waved his baton and the band jumped into the up-tempo Homeland Helper Show theme music.

The principal hurried back to open the door.

She smiled and waved the cast and mayor and wife inside.

As they walked onto the stage the crowd stood to clap and cheer.

"Yaay!"

For several moments the cast and crowd crouched and pointed back and forth.

Rosey and her group stood for a while in the back and then dispersed.

The band played the national anthem and the principal led the crowd in the Our Sun God.

She then introduced each of the cast members, in turn, to the squeals and snapshots and screams of the crowd and the press.

"H-O-M-E-L-A-N-D!" The cast members led the crowd in a pep rally, each holding up a letter glued with their publicity photo on a piece of hard board.

"And now," began one of the lovely young male cast members, "*your* newly *re*-elected mayor — Dick Heavens! Oh, my!"

Dick took the microphone.

"Thank you, Tommie.

"And thank you!"

He crouched and pointed a finger at the crowd.

"All of you gathered right here today and also those everywhere in radio and television land!"

He pointed at one of the TV cameras and the local radio announcer in the front row.

"And most of all, thank you, thank you, thank you, to those who have taken the time from their busy work week to register for *The* Homeland Home Helper Show segment drawing!"

# The American Dream

He raised a clenched fist and the crowd rose and clapped their hands over their heads.

"Yaaay!"

"This fall," Dick began, and the crowd stood again to cheer.

He bid them to sit with an open hand pressed gently downward.

"This fall, The Home Helper Show is coming to Homeland!"

The crowd stood and cheered.

"To film a special!"

And again all stood.

"This is an All-American city. The All-American town!"

"This is why they are coming here.

"We are The American Dream.

"We live in The American Dream.

"The American Dream is what we are about.

"It's what allows us to keep going."

He looked down, stepped slightly forward and lowered his voice.

"They will not stop us.

"They want to paralyze us.

"We will improve our lives.

"We will water. We will mow.

"We will get better and better ... and better."

"Yaaay!"

"And ..." Dick put a finger into the air and the crowd clapped and yelled and stomped their feet.

M also stood and clapped and stomped and yelled.

His little girl looked back at him over her mother's shoulder and waved.

M waved back.

"Dick! Dick! Dick!" they chanted.

"And ..." He raised a finger again to quiet the people.

"The epitome of The American Dream is ... The American Home!"

"Yaay! Dick!"

"And a pool!

"And a larger kitchen!

"And another bathroom downstairs!"

"Yaaay! Yaay!"

"And now ...

"It's time to find out just what Homeland American Family is going to be on The Home Helper Show this fall!

"Jane?"

Jane stepped up and Dick handed her the microphone.

"Jane! Jane! Jane!" The crowd remained standing to chant.

The HH cast pushed out a giant triple-piece see-through toaster, on wheels, filled with the thousands of hopeful registration cards just waiting to identify the host family for the house makeover.

Jane grabbed the handle and rolled it over and over.

The crowd stopped chanting and clapping, and stood mute, hands over mouths and hearts, unable to breathe.

Jane stopped the toaster from rolling; the mass of cards flopped one last time.

Someone dropped car keys, and a baby cried out.

A dog barked outside, and somewhere the school custodians complained to each other about something.

Jane opened the gate.

She shoved her hand into the cards, and kept tunneling, up to her shoulder.

# The American Dream

She came out with one card in her hand and held it above her head.

Jane came to the very front of the stage, stood straight and blonde. She held the microphone and the card in front of her face.

She smiled.

She read the card.

She ceased smiling.

"Umm," said Jane. She looked back at Dick. He nodded to her to hurry the fuck up.

"Uh," Jane put the microphone closer to her mouth.

"Umm, Michael M," she mumbled. "Mrs. M?"

"What?"

"What'd she say?"

"Who?"

"Speak up! C'mon, Jane, who won!"

"The Michael M family. The M's are the winner!" she shouted.

Mrs. M swayed and nearly fell as the crowd hummed, sighed, moaned and sat, in turn.

"Well, he's not here." Dick moved up to stand next to Jane.

He took the microphone from Jane.

"He has to be here to be eligible — official rules. He's not here. We'll draw again. Jane?"

He took Jane's hand to bring her back to the toaster.

"I am. Here."

M stood and removed his gray felt hat.

His family looked back at him. His wife turned away, facing the stage. His daughter reached out to him. He stretched to hold her little hand.

# Mike Palecek

M's wife stood and turned around again, shoving aside a metal folding chair with her foot so that he could come up to stand with his family.

"We are here!" He grabbed his wife's hand and raised it.

M picked up his children, one on his shoulders and the other in one arm. He gripped his wife's sweaty hand with the other.

They walked down the row, then up the center aisle.

Their steps and their breathing echoed in the gym.

They climbed the stairs to the stage and stood, gleaming, with the Home Helper cast and Dick and Jane. The television cameras zoomed and photographers clicked and flashed.

The band played the Home Helper theme music.

The cast moved the M family in between Dick and Jane, their arms around each other. They all crouched and pointed fingers at the cameras and crowd.

The principal retrieved the microphone from Dick's limp hand and began to thank everyone for coming.

"Make sure to watch Home Helper this fall ... every ..."

Just then the music stopped in mid-measure and four men with Down's Syndrome, wearing green and black camouflage fatigues and orange face paint, appeared behind the group on stage.

The men held toy black and green automatic weapons and paintball guns pointed at Dick and Jane and the others.

More of Rosey's friends appeared at the back and side doors, blocking egress.

A door opened and slammed.

Rosey The Riveter promenaded in from the cafeteria door, slowly, smiling, wearing a cocked black beret. Her T-shirt featured the black outline of M's profile sporting a sparse beard and beret.

# The American Dream

Rosey sauntered up with a WWF swagger and smirk. Her T-shirt was rolled to her shoulder. She held up her arm and posed, showing her muscle.

"Thank you," she said, removing the microphone from the principal's hand.

Rosey stepped in front of the on-stage group to address the crowd, stuck to their metal chairs by freeze-dried sweat.

"Good morning!

"Greetings!

"Ho-la!

"The American Dream, indeed. Oh, Jesus.

"Set your alarm.

"Wake up!"

She looked left and right and down and to the back, smiling, waving at relatives, then gritted her teeth.

"You! You! You!" she pointed at people she knew: a woman checker from the grocery, the bank teller, the football assistant coach.

"*Do* something!

"Hey!"

The crowd jumped back in their seats and pulled their hands to their chests.

Americans are guilty as sin, says the Nuremburg thing, for not doing anything.

"Bank accounts, people starving. Guilty!

"Stealing. Guilty!

"Lying. Guilty.

"War, Murder, Greed. Ignorance. Guilty-guilty.

"Apathy."

Should I go on?

"Yes!" yelled two people in the back.

158

"Silence."

Rosey took a deep breath and looked toward the rear open door.

"And we will now ask the big, dark, handsome United Nations soccer player soldiers, in those robin's egg blue helmets, waiting in the troop carriers surrounding this block, ...

"Please come in and take these fucking Americans away, out of our sight — to trial, to prison, to exile, to cry, some to commit suicide no doubt, some most assuredly to execution."

She held the microphone at her side and watched the back door.

The crowd sat silent.

Freedom Fizz ran in a stream down the middle aisle.

Someone coughed, and someone could be heard crying while searching for her keys in her big purse.

Dick inched away toward the door. A man named Marvin, wearing gray and blue face paint and a Dallas Cowboys stocking cap, shoved a toy AK-47 into his stomach and said, "I don't think so."

Rosey watched the back door without expression, stone faced.

She dropped the microphone to the floor, sending a chilling echo squeaking through the giant room.

"We're going to be tortured!" screamed a woman to her husband.

"Oh, brother," said Rosey.

"What a bunch of retards.

"Go fuck yourselves."

She nodded to her people on the stage and at the doors and they melted away.

M squeezed his wife's shoulders tightly and kissed her on the lips, then crouched down to hug his kids.

# The American Dream

A dog barked down the street, the yips drifting in through the open back door of the gym. A few school custodians reached for long brooms, and Principal Campbell began to whisper in the ears of the Homeland Helper cast that she would like to take them all out to lunch.

With clenched fist held high above her head, Rosey marched to the end of the stage, down the steps, up the center aisle and out the back door.

Dick and Jane walked over and stood behind "Soup" Campbell until the principal invited them along to Penelope's.

Rosey met with her comrades in the parking lot across from the elementary. They exchanged knuckle taps and walked together toward the gas station on the highway for SuperSize pops.

Dark clouds rolled in, almost rubbing their bellies on the treetops.

Michael M, his wife and kids were getting their T-shirts autographed by the Home Helper cast. The janitors had divided the gym into sixths for cleanup duty. They stood in the back, leaning on their brooms, staring at people to make them leave.

Pastor Steve Cash ushered his family out with both arms, heading up the middle aisle of the elementary school gym.

John the Baptist switched off his radio, walked into the bathroom, did his business and flushed.

A man sitting on his haunches in the sun on Main Street jerked his head in the direction of the school. A helicopter pushed off from the landing pad at Git Mo's.


The driver of a mini-van on the highway pointed out to his family a black cloud, pouring from the elm trees in the middle of Homeland.

Neighbor ladies, visiting out of doors in the Freedom and Liberty area, held up their arms to dodge a falling walker, a

## Mike Palecek

Baby Doll, a huge stroller, a bent BJ hood and the bottom plate of a denture.

Burning chunks, like toddler steaks on a backyard grill, splashed sizzling into the city pool.

Bits of brick and mortar and metal and wood rained back down upon the earth, all around the bookstore, the jail, the dentist office. Workers hurried outside to look up into the sky, squinting against the pelting droplets.

Lightning cracked, and the flagpole atop Sun God Reformed Church toppled, taking off a corner of the building. The clean white flag plopped into a puddle of mud.

A siren cried. It wavered, wailed, howled and echoed, bouncing off the buildings, running up and down the hot cement roads, around the homes, through the backyards, searching for the children.

Mothers on the Eastside and the Westside counted heads inside their frazzled brains. They wiped hands down aprons, preparing to spring into action.

An owl hooted at seeing a motley cat leap over a yawning lion.

The Rapture horn atop the Community Center screamed out bloody murder.

The train whistle tooted and the blood and molten bone poured from the elementary school gym, into the scorched cement street, like strawberry ice cream.

Above the town, behind the post office, across the alley from the library, the sun shone down on Homeland's water tower. It was a shaft of pure light, Jacob's Ladder, by which they could almost reach paradise.

A group of second graders looked down from the walkway, watching the burning elementary school.

They stood gripping the railing, buckets of dripping red paint and brushes at their feet, paint in their hair and on their arms and faces and clothes.

Behind them the newly painted shiny gray water tower had just received another coat: "No War".

# NO
# WAR

The children licked at
tears.

They scrunched up their
faces to try to stop crying.

Two of the children, a dark-
haired boy and a blonde
girl, hugged each other and
then sat, bare feet dangling
in mid-air, swinging.

Below them on the ground
by their overturned bicycles
lay their fishing poles and
slingshots and straw hats.

# Epilogue

They call us tinfoil hat wearin' kooks.
What about the jet planes flyin' all around
While 'our' mighty air defenses were standin' down?
They say that we should blindly believe 'our'
government.

Before you start preaching
Let me ask you this my friend.

Have you forgotten
What we saw as one?
Oh, those towers turned to dust
They were blown to kingdom come

Have you forgotten
Just how fast they fell?
Office fires can't do that
No, there ain't no way in hell.

And you try to blame it all
upon Bin Laden

Have you forgotten
They destroyed the molten metal
From the WTC.
It's too incriminating
For you to see

That would blow the cover
That would solve the crime
The biggest inside job
Of all time

Some see a police state
Comin' into view
After 9/11 man
I'd have to say that's true.
The 'confession tape'
Looks nothing like bin Laden

Have you forgotten?
They got their new Pearl Harbor
To justify their wars
The power and the money
That's what they did it for

Have you forgotten
All the people killed?
As the empire marches on
Down to the oil fields

Have you forgotten
About 'our' Pentagon
All the loved ones that we lost
To the Neo-Cons
Face the truth

Forget about bin Laden

Have you forgotten?
Have you forgotten?

– Ace Baker, "Blown to Kingdom Come"

166

Mike Palecek

# About The Author

Mike Palecek is:

> a former federal prisoner for peace
>
> a small-town newspaper reporter, editor and publisher
>
> the Iowa Democratic Party nominee for
> Congress, Fifth District, 2000

In 1979, Mike attended St. John Vianney, a Catholic seminary on campus at the College of St. Thomas, St. Paul, Minnesota. He left seminary in 1980 to go to New York City and volunteer at The Catholic Worker, on the Bowery. During the 1980s the Paleceks lived in a resistance community in north Omaha.

Mike was arrested several times at Offutt Air Force base, and served five jail terms: ten days, thirty days, fifty days, six months, six months. He served time at Douglas County Jail [Omaha], Sarpy County [Papillion, Nebr.], Lancaster County [Lincoln, Nebr.], Pottawatamie County [Council Bluffs, Iowa], Metropolitan Correctional Center [Chicago], Terre Haute Penitentiary [Terre Haute, Indiana], Leavenworth Penitentiary [Leavenworth, Kansas], El Reno Federal Correctional Institution [El Reno, Oklahoma], Midland, Texas city jail and the La Tuna FCI [El Paso, Texas].

Mike became clinically depressed his last time in jail (the six-month stint in the Council Bluffs jail). Perhaps it was due to post-traumatic stress from previous jail time, combined with missing his two-year-old son. He left the life of civil disobedience and went into journalism, working at small newspapers in Nebraska, Minnesota and Iowa and receiving various writing and photography awards.

While working at a weekly newspaper in the Nebraska Sandhills Mike wrote a column against the first Gulf War titled *I don't support the troops*. His column was cancelled, the family was threatened and they left to find their own paper.

# Mike Palecek

The tiny newspaper Ruth and Mike ran in the early '90s in southeast Minnesota won the Newspaper of the Year Award from the Minnesota Newspaper Association. The paper went out of business later that year.

Mike worked as a reporter, editor and publisher at the Ainsworth [Neb.] Star-Journal, Byron [MN] Review, Cherokee [IA] Daily Times, and the N'West Iowa Review. He also wrote for the Sioux Falls Argus Leader, Rochester Post-Bulletin, Norfolk Daily News and The National Catholic Reporter

Palecek ran for the U.S. House of Representatives in 2000 and won the nomination of the Iowa Democratic Party for the Fifth District. As part of his campaign, he walked from his home in Sheldon to the IRS office in Sioux City, a one week walk, to turn in a crossed-out tax form saying he would not pay for war,

He received over 65,000 votes in a conservative district on an anti-prison, anti-military, pro-Hispanic immigration platform.

In a previous run as a write-in candidate he walked from the Air National Guard Base in Sioux City to the base in Fort Dodge to protest Clinton's bombing of Yugoslavia.

Palecek left newspaper work in 1997 to concentrate on novels.

# About The Cover Artist

Food Not Bombs co-founder, Keith McHenry was born in Frankfurt, West Germany in 1957 while his father was stationed there in the army. His ancestors include a signer of the United States Constitution who also served as a general in the Revolutionary War and, as Secretary of War under George Washington, founded the U.S. military. Other famous ancestors include Bob and Charlie Ford, who joined Jesse James' gang in 1882 and killed the famous train robber for a $10,000 reward.

Keith studied painting at Boston University and in 1979, he started an advertising firm in Boston. He designed calendars, ads, and brochures for the Boston Celtics, the Boston Red Sox, the Environmental Protection Agency, and a multitude of commercial and alternative businesses. He won several Clio Awards for his designs. His anti-nuclear war street art became the subject of an Off Broadway play called *Murder Now!* and a film called *The Sidewalk Sector.*

In 1980, Keith and seven friends created Food Not Bombs. After eight years of serving free food and doing graphic arts work in Boston, Keith moved to San Francisco where he started a second Food Not Bombs group. Since then, Keith has been arrested over 100 times for serving free food in city parks and he has spent over 500 nights in jail. In 1995 Amnesty International and the United Nations Human Rights Commission joined thousands of supporter in working for his release. He faced 25 years to life after being framed under the California Three Strikes Law, because of his Food Not Bombs work.

McHenry also co-authored and illustrated the book Food Not Bombs: How to Feed the Hungry and Build Community which has sold more than 10,000 copies in four languages. The 20th Anniversary English edition was published in Tucson by See Sharp Press.

His work with Food Not Bombs also appeared in the 1995 *Amnesty International Human Rights Report,* No Trespassing by Anders Corr, Interviews With Icons by Lisa Law and A People's History of the United States by Howard Zinn. There is a chapter about him in 50 American Revolutions You're Not Supposed to Know by Mickey Z. His work on the UnFree Trade Tour was detailed in Por el Reparto del Trabajo y la Riqueza by Jose Iglesias Fernandez published in Madrid, Spain.

Recipient of numerous awards, he has also received attention from the government because of his outspoken views. In 2004 he helped organize a protest against torture; in 2005 NBC-TV reported that the Pentagon classified the action as an on-going, creditable terrorist threat. According to internal government documents the FBI's Joint Terrorism Task Force has been investigating and disrupting Food Not Bombs groups in Arizona, California, Colorado, Texas, North Carolina and many other states.

Keith has visited Food Not Bombs groups all over Europe, the Middle East, Africa and the Americas. The last time Keith flew into the United States he was met at the door of the plane by two Homeland Security officers who searched his bags and wallet while questioning him about his work with Food Not Bombs and the peace movement. One of the officers typed in information from the contents of his wallet into a Homeland Security computer. There have been several reports that Food Not Bombs is listed on the FBI's "Terrorist Watch List" .

# About The Publisher

I am founding CWG Press because I love books and I see many that deserve to be published, but that are not getting into print. Sometimes this happens because the material is too controversial for a mainstream publisher. Sometimes it's because a particular book probably won't appeal to a mass market. Sometimes it's happenstance, because it can be very hard to find a publisher willing to take a chance.

That is why there is room for CWG Press. That is why there is a need for CWG Press.

I will select books based on quality. I will publish books that I have been lucky enough to encounter, that are worthy of being shared with the world. I will do the very best that I can to select good books, prepare them, publicize them, and distribute them.

If you don't like the books I publish, you can blame me for picking them—although I don't guarantee that even I will *like* every book that I publish. As I said before, selection of books will be based on quality, not merely personal preference.

If you like the books I publish, you can compliment me on finding them (please do!), but the real praise should of course be extended to the authors. All I am doing is providing a stage to showcase their accomplishments. The writers have the creative genius—I'm just helping them express it to the world.

I have already mentioned the world twice in this mission statement. It's not by chance. Freedom has no borders, no nationality. Freedom starts within each one of us, and extends to everyone, whether or not we agree with their views or their methods. I will restrict no one's freedom to express ideas. I will not accept anyone's interference with my freedom. There will be no censorship at CWG Press.

Is CWG Press a religious press?  A Christian Press, perhaps?  No--but I will publish Christian books, or Muslim books, or any other religious—or atheist--books, if they are of good quality.

Is CWG Press a political press?  Does it strive for social change?  No--although I personally strive for social change.  I will publish political books of good quality, whether or not I agree with them, because above all I believe in freedom of the press.  Let the ideas fight it out in the public forum--it's not right for me to selectively publish only books that have the same viewpoint as I do.

Is CWG Press a free press?  Yes, yes, emphatically yes ... although I am not in a position to publish free books.

# Books By Mike Palecek

## Fiction:

Killing George Bush, Publish America

Joe Coffee's Revolution, Badger Books

Twins, Badger Books

The Truth, New Hampshire Writers Collective

The Last Liberal Outlaw, New Leaf

Looking For Bigfoot, Howling Dog Press

Terror Nation, Mainstay Press

The American Dream, CWG Press [Spring '07]

## Non-fiction:

Prophets Without Honor, Algora Publishing (with William
  Strabala)

Mike Palecek

# The American Dream

# About The Book

The American Dream was written by Mike Palecek in 2006.

Editing and design were performed by Chuck Gregory of CWG Press, Fort Lauderdale, using the excellent open-source program OpenOffice.org.

Printed by Peer Print, Fort Lauderdale.

ISBN 0-9788186-0-1

51595>

9 780978 818609